Necessary Lies

ALSO BY JANICE DAUGHARTY

Dark of the Moon
Going Through the Change

Necessary
Lies

A NOVEL

Janice
Daugharty

HarperCollins*Publishers*

HarperCollins books may be purchased for educational, business, or sales pro-
motional use. For information please write: Special Markets Department,
HarperCollins Publishers, Inc., 10 East 53rd Street, New York, NY 10022.

FIRST EDITION

Designed by Alma Hochhauser Orenstein

Library of Congress Cataloging-in-Publication Data

Daugharty, Janice, 1944–
   Necessary lies : a novel / Janice Daugharty — 1st ed.
      p. cm.
   ISBN 0-06-017177-4
   I. Title.
PS3554.A844N43 1995
813'.54—dc20   94-18745

95 96 97 98 99 ❖/HC 10 9 8 7 6 5 4 3 2 1

For Nancy Zimmerman and Susan Ramer,
who hovered over this manuscript till
Larry Ashmead could harvest it as a book.
And especially for my family.

Who are these coming to the sacrifice?
To what green altar, O mysterious priest, Lead'st thou that
heifer lowing at the skies,
And all her silken flanks with garlands drest? What little town
by river or sea shore Or mountain-built with peaceful citadel,
Is emptied of this folk, this pious morn? And, little town, thy
streets for evermore Will silent be; and not a soul to tell
Why thou art desolate, can e'er return.

JOHN KEATS, "ODE ON A GRECIAN URN"

1

One of the last to leave stopped at the door and shook the preacher's hand, going on about the sermon in a familiar wheedling tone, and Brother Leroy's cautious laugh wended back into the sanctuary, relief telling in the sound of a sigh. Then wearily he strolled toward the pulpit and, spying Cliffie, seemed surprised, but said only, "Cliffie!," head hung as in a recapitulation of believing that the long Sunday had ceased. He stopped at the altar and stared at her.

Shambling out between pews, she blurted, "I'm gonna have a baby," and watched for shock to register on his mercurial face. "Roy Harris's," she added. "He don't want to get married." She'd waited so long—it seemed years—for a way out to ripen with time, and now that her secret was said, she felt sapped.

Leaning against the altar table, Brother Leroy shrank, whole body, like somebody dead whose soul is withdrawing with his breath. "Why, Cliffie!" he said in that detached squeak of a voice, always used when, even knowing better, he hoped to stave off a full confession, as though in not knowing all he might be spared, being not God but man and ultimately without that power they all believed him to possess.

She waited with him while his blue eyes glazed over and he thought her news through, or maybe banked it by the numerous possibilities adrift in that unsullied holy mind where sins-of-others came and went and scarred: none of his, theirs, his cross. Like a dead man, waxen and bloodless, he seemed to tally up those possibilities and the futility of it all, to dredge deep for strength and answers, and finding none, reached back, as though with the hand of another—a hand not at all accustomed to dipping into the collection plate (he always insisted that one of the deacons collect the money, as he always insisted that each sister and brother confess to God instead of the preacher)—and took from the offering a couple of bills, which somehow ended up a ten and a five.

He stared at the bouquet of bills and appeared to be vowing not to think, but to act—alone, without God present—and handed it to Cliffie. Then bending, blue shirt brightening in a print of angel wings across his sweaty shoulder blades, he tore a scrap of paper from a sack of new red potatoes, an alternative offering. Nervously, he flattened the scrap on the table and scribbled, then passed it on to Cliffie too.

"Go to her," he said, tapping the paper with his pen. "You can walk there, Cliffie—back behind the schoolhouse in the quarters. Go to her, first thing." He talked through his teeth and shuddered, holy-wan face alight with wonder at himself, and seemed to steel against an inner quaking from the Lord. "Oh, Lord, have mercy on us all!" He gazed up at the ceiling, where the old lanterns shed a heavenly white light on it all: the situation and possibilities, the weak human condition that spells itself in sin. "She'll take care of you."

All the time Cliffie had been standing there she'd been waiting for a solution and thought at first that he meant her to go to a doctor. But on the scrap of paper sack she read the name "Witch Seymour." Cliffie had heard of the Negro woman who'd earned the name "Witch" for her potions, which usually worked, but if they failed, she went in there. That's how the tobacco hands had put it, telling of Clorox dosing and douching, and as a last resort, a coat hanger.

Hot bile rising in her throat, Cliffie pinned the preacher

with her eyes. She'd believed that surely, if he didn't fix things, he might offer some advice, as her Sunday-school book said. If not a miracle, anything but filching from the collection plate—an abomination—and offering the name of a butcher. She wadded the bills with the paper scrap and hurled it at his feet.

From the front stoop, she canvassed the open church grounds, where children spirited like untold demons in the dusk and grown-ups formed into puddlelike shadows, the smell of night coming thick and tart from the pine woods. She always hated that feeling of having been there before, of having looked out on the same scene a thousand and one Sundays, and to her absolute horror, this time she didn't. This time stood out. Time stopped.

Oh, God, she'd told Brother Leroy! Had she really expected him to make Roy Harris marry her, maybe ease the news to Pappy Ocain, who was so down on the daddy of her baby? She picked out Pappy Ocain and Maude, talking with another couple beneath the black gum tree by the pumphouse, then crept down the doorsteps. Forcing each step through on locked quivering knees, she kept her eyes on Pappy Ocain's battered green pickup. It was parked on the grass shoulder of the dirt lane that led from the woods road to the church. She didn't know how she'd make it that far, weak as she was, but the truck looked like home, a place to go inside and get it all back together again, but also like Pappy Ocain, tilted, wronged. His truck.

Yesterday, she'd discovered that she had outgrown them both. Following a two-day rain that burgeoned the creeks and ditches, she had gone out riding the dirt roads with Pappy Ocain, checking for fish, for places to set out his wire baskets. A long day in the tobacco-fumed truck, lost in her thoughts, with him eying her between stops in the dead flatwoods springing to life with reddening maples and greening gums.

He seemed to know, but what he knew was not what she knew, the real reason behind why she could no longer go out riding with him the way she used to. "What say we go on back to the house?" he'd said. "Big girl like you mought wanta be listening to the radio." Then he turned on the radio to crackling static and kept riding as if to show her he knew what he didn't know, what would change them forever when he did.

Night lights flickered on, beaming down from each corner of the church eaves, and glanced off the bug-frosted windshield of the truck, blinding the inside. Good—she could faint in private, if indeed she was about to faint. The ringing of locusts loaded the air, and her ears felt stopped up.

While tipping toward the truck, she listened hard to the burble of odd talk from groups about the yard to hear if anybody had noticed her. For balance, she focused on the grille of the truck, where a dead bird was bradded to the metal grid. Stiff, its wings molded to the surface, tiny round head backflung, resisting, beak and eyes rimmed a sour blue. The finest down under the black feathers trembled in the warm air. It smelled faintly of the first stages of rot, warm and milk-ripe, not yet foul but vulnerable.

Suddenly, she felt overcome with the need to cry, a warm fluid rush in her chest that gathered in her face. Poor bird! Poor baby! Poor Cliffie! She could look for that hypocrite preacher to march straight from the church and tell Pappy Ocain any minute now. She eased the truck door open and slid in and closed it with only a snib of the latch. A thin whine of mosquitoes wreathed her head, so she rolled up the window to keep more from collecting and to filter the siren of brats swooping from the dark cemetery behind the church to the lit sand of the front yard.

Cliffie hoped they'd play a long time; she hoped Pappy Ocain and Maude would talk a long time. Give her bleeding heart time to clot. Tears sprang to her eyeballs and just as quickly drained behind them. She had adopted that trick out of necessity; she had no privacy, and if anyone in her family should catch her crying, they wouldn't let up till they learned what was wrong. All of it.

Resting her head against the cool window glass, she watched Pappy Ocain shift feebly in the gutted shadows of the black gum. "Ain't the skeeters bad this evening?" he said and slapped his arm, hand raking down. His full-legged khakis made his frail legs look sturdy. But his white shins were sharp as a bar of whittled lye; Cliffie had seen them in summer when he sat on the porch with his pants legs rolled.

Would he kill Roy Harris? She tucked a foot beneath her and groaned. She didn't know. She had grown up disbelieving the rumor about Pappy Ocain's shooting off his own finger— his trigger finger—to keep from killing again after he got saved. It was something she lived with, the rumor, that he didn't know she knew. At times she did wonder about the rumor, having gone beyond that stage when she found the anomaly of that hand fascinating rather than freakish. She used to sit beside him on the porch and play with that stump of finger, a pinkish shirr of skin, that same finger she had held to when he would walk her up the lane from the house to Cornerville to show her off at the post office or the store.

And stretching her recall to before the loss of that finger, she could call up an image of that fiercer, slicker Ocain and his foxy retaliation on anybody who crossed him, and through Cliffie, him. He had stepped over that line from lost to saved, or so it seemed in her head, when she had turned six or seven, as evidenced by the sudden loss of that finger she'd gripped leaving the beauty contest at school. And she could still feel that finger wrapped in her small hand as they had left the darkened school grounds in the chirrup of frogs and the shrill of katydids, swirly shadows under the great live oaks. She in a cut-down silky purple dress of Maude's, with lipstick on her lips that made them feel sticky, and he in his best chinos with one pants leg stuffed in his black boot. A tiny girl with glossy blond curls and a hoop-skirted, pink net dress had won the beauty contest because her daddy was on the board of education, and Pappy Ocain hated her. Or maybe her daddy. Cliffie wasn't sure, but she was sure that Pappy Ocain didn't hate her for losing.

His boots slapped hard on the dirt of the school grounds as he tugged her along, spitting and spouting about how Cliffie was the prettiest, how by rights she should have won. Somebody had paid off the judges. That bunch at the courthouse. And at the school gate, he had turned toward town instead of home, and they were off to Cornerville, where lights burned dim in the row of houses from the school to the courthouse, high, white, and leaning into the moonless night. And there she'd helped Pappy Ocain gather rocks and sticks to throw at the courthouse windows and listened to the chimes of shattering glass, him laughing and hooting like a mean man she'd dreamed in black and white.

He seemed so restrained now, as if something inside had been buried. Her mama, too: soft, silent, mechanical, spooning mashed green peas to the next-to-the-youngest's mouth. Nursing the baby—often alternating between babies—she'd nibble the tiny fingernails, her face furrowing, distant, content. Both she and Pappy Ocain close to sixty: farmed-out, rutted-out, numb, acquiescent.

Cliffie had never thought about going to her mama with her secret. Maude was the property of the baby, or babies, until they got old enough to wander off to school. That's when Pappy Ocain took over, quietly sitting aside on one end of the porch, chewing tobacco and spitting, cracking pointless remarks as the older children came and went, going about their own business, earning their own way when they tired of sweet potatoes, greens, and corn bread, sidemeat and grits.

"Y'all as welcome as the flowers in May to what we got, and thank the Lord above for it," he'd say. "With me ailing like I am . . ." Trailing off, he would gaze out over the broom-sage fields, as though he would if he could, and they never quite knew what he would do if he could, only that in the pushed-back past he had farmed and now did nothing. Worn-out foot propped on the porch post, he'd go on about how he'd walked a many a mile behind a mule, breaking ground in the flatwoods that broke him.

He never mentioned the welfare checks that started in 1950, three years before, in support of his not-working with a bad heart. Neither were the checks mentioned by the children, who brought them home from the post office in Cornerville, a half mile west of the house. Not that they feared mentioning the checks, they just understood his fierce, disjointed pride.

But Cliffie appreciated the unmentionable checks, because the churches would no longer feel compelled to take up love offerings for them every fifth Sunday. And although she still went to school at Swanoochee County High, eleventh grade, with those who attended the Cornerville Baptist Church, Pappy Ocain had moved their membership to the church in the flatwoods at Needmore, a shut-down sawmill town. Pappy Ocain believed in membership and moved theirs often.

It was from the church in the flatwoods that Cliffie first slipped off with Roy Harris Weeks. But she'd already got to know him from school, and knew of him before that. Like a slow heat building to a boil, Pappy Ocain had started warning Cliffie and her sisters to steer clear of Roy Harris Weeks, and as she and Mary Helen got bigger, filling out, he'd built up to daring them even to look that no-account's way. Why? Pappy Ocain never said, never had to say anything, just laid down the laws for them to go by. But it was no real mystery. Cliffie knew Roy Harris's bad side. (She was now seventeen and he was mysteriously older; she didn't know how much older, and his age seemed significant only in that it was a mystery.)

Attending school off and on, or as Roy Harris would say,

"when the mood strikes me," he'd appeared to simply taper to more off-days than on during that last year. When he had gone, he was like a magnet dragged along the halls of the lofty old schoolhouse, attracting girls like roofing tacks. He was crusty and aloof, dashingly dastard.

Cliffie had known all along—and now could admit—that the girls Roy Harris attracted were not of the nice-girl class she aspired to. Also she had known—and now accepted as fact—that with or without her choice to associate with Roy Harris, she never would have fit in that class. She couldn't have made herself up enough, or altered the quality of her voice enough—though she tried—to meet their standards. Her face burned, recalling having tried to chum with Lanie Herndon, Cheryl Mosely, the others.

The very name "Cliffie," as with all the names in her family, revealed who she was and where she came from. She didn't even have a name until she was going on two. Her brother Scooter, who had named himself after a smart red scooter in the Sears catalog, had kept ragging her about her bangs sticking out like a cliff, and the name had stuck.

She thought about her four older brothers, who were seldom home, and how they'd steal from the house with their moon-pale hair slicked from long grave faces. They all looked down as they strolled up the lane, en route to somewhere that made up their lives. Oddly, they never went to church with Cliffie and the others, and she wondered if it was because there was not enough room in the truck, or because they didn't want to go, whether at some point the Flowers children became independent enough to simply refuse. Maybe Pappy Ocain's firm control over his children fizzled when they got to a certain size. Or maybe the boys did as they pleased because they were boys. (K.C., Cliffie's younger brother, still went to church, but wasn't under Pappy Ocain's rule like the girls.)

So many halfway marks in my world, Cliffie thought,

thinking about the halfway mark of her age—neither woman nor child. And there certainly seemed to be a transitional midpoint between the boys and the girls in the family: ten divided by two. Five girls, all told, including the two babies, the older ones fairer and more passionate than the boys. Especially Cliffie. Her sisters had an innocuously coarse texture and not a trace of insight. They were quiet only when they sulked. Their mouths never closed; even at night they talked in their sleep, smacking overblown lips.

That irked Cliffie, who slightly resembled them, who possessed the best of their traits, the worst traits, she liked to think, almost refined out in her. She knew she must protect herself, must guard against those undesirable traits that could flourish and overtake her. All of them had a tendency toward stout hips and legs. So far, Cliffie's were nicely rounded. Too much fatback and dried limas and she'd be doomed.

She never allowed her long blond hair the freedom to frizz. She learned to lightly tuck her lips. Her thick nose could be thinned by a process called "shadowing," which she'd read about in a fashion magazine in the school library. She'd also learned to shave her legs with Pappy Ocain's razor, which was stored in a filmy jelly glass on the back-porch water shelf, from *Seventeen* magazine (they didn't tell how to conceal bloody trickling nicks). She'd read the articles too, excavating more and more of those fascinating magazines, and learned that it was typical to be pouty. She fell in love with being typical, vowed she would always be. In love, too. You couldn't be a typical teen and not be in love. But the choice of boys was so slim in her little circle—church, the only place Pappy Ocain allowed them to go, except school, where the boys were dull and lacking, compared to Roy Harris. Any one of which Pappy Ocain would have picked instead.

She certainly couldn't go back to school in September in her shape. She would be in maternity clothes by then. She shuddered, picturing herself like Maude with the last baby, hard belly bound in a white elastic inset that showed beneath a flared smock, as she'd waddle along the halls, Cheryl Mosely and them giggling in a huddle.

Ever since she'd met Roy Harris, Cliffie had felt her ideals slipping away, passion taking over, her thoughts swapping sides. Even if she weren't pregnant, she probably would quit school, like her older brothers. State law permitted quitting at sixteen, but Cliffie had hung in there to keep from disappointing Pappy Ocain. But she'd thought a lot about quitting, during the last coast-along year, and how, symbolically, she would drift easterly to the flatwoods, like the cloud toward Canaan, where people with no more ambition than herself were scattered along dirt roads, throughout the pine woods, instead of trailing west to nearby Cornerville, where life was ordered. Still a little town, separating itself by the Alapaha River from the larger civilization of Georgia, Cornerville was ordered by institutions and calibrations, such as a school and a courthouse, a post office and a health department.

Cliffie twisted around on the truck seat, feet flat on the floor. She didn't really know what it would take to put her life on the right course, respectably married to Roy Harris Weeks and off with him to Fort Bragg. Though the word "respectable" didn't quite mesh with the role of Mrs. Roy Harris Weeks. Sometimes she wrote the name in the dirt at home, quickly erasing it so nobody would see. She would be amazed at how the love she'd felt for Roy Harris hadn't really lasted as long as she'd expected—forever. And how ironic that she was now in the throes of trying to piece together a lifetime with him. But she really didn't have all that many other choices: she could run away alone and without a dime, stay home and have the baby and end up like her mama, or go to Witch Seymour.

What she wished was she'd never gone all the way with Roy Harris. But she had, and now she had to go one step further. Single, she would be scandalized; married, she'd be saved. Even so, she really hated to disappoint Pappy Ocain, who'd always believed in her, had such high hopes. If only he'd get to know Roy Harris—well, maybe not. But she couldn't help feeling sorry for Roy Harris, stranded out there in the flatwoods with his foster mother and her afflicted children. Aunt Teat, as everybody called her, had taken Roy Harris in, according to him, because she needed the money to help out with her own three children. And sometimes he even helped tend them, but he was cynical, angry, determined to separate himself. Off to Fort Bragg.

Cliffie never blamed him for his distaste for Aunt Teat, who invited pity, even deserved it, had she not begged. Cliffie understood his attitude, being fifth in a family of ten children herself—deprived, responsible, handy. But in comparison to his family, her own dull-eyed brothers and sisters appeared healthy, her mama and daddy proud and presentable. Who could fault him for always threatening to hop the next freight train to switch tracks in Needmore? But she did fault him for trying to skip out on his own baby.

This morning, when she'd slipped from church to meet him at Aunt Teat's house in the woods, he'd put her off, scratched his head and said, "I don't know. I'm bound for Fort Bragg Monday week."

"But I . . . ," Cliffie said aloud inside the truck, catching herself saying what she'd said that morning, what she'd been saying regularly for months, and cut it off. She bit her lip, hating Roy Harris, somewhere across the woods right now—with all her heart she hated him, right now, and wished Pappy Ocain and them would come on to the truck while she was good and mad.

Peering out the window at the buzzing huddle beneath the black gum, Cliffie recognized Mary Helen's thick, squarish silhouette, behind Pappy Ocain and Maude. And just when did she pop up there? And where was that blabbermouth while Cliffie was talking to Brother Leroy? The roots of her hair tightened.

She watched as Brother Leroy's wife, Sister Mary, appeared in the spill of light from the door of the Sunday-school wing, their two little boys hovering close. Herding them onward, she glided wraithlike behind, pausing to speak to one of the women beneath the black gum—their voices an attenuating song on the night—and on toward the parsonage, adjacent to the church.

Cliffie couldn't think of Sister Mary in any way but sick— the two boys too, predisposed to languishing. She'd stayed with them off and on all winter, free of charge, while they had flu, so Brother Leroy could get out and visit the sick and peddle his greens, eggs, and junk iron. Cliffie shuddered, recalling having spent a large part of her time last winter in that bleak place.

The parsonage, really nothing but a shanty, sat in the clearing of flatwoods, dense for miles around with pines and palmettos, scrub oaks and gums. Actually, the preacher's place was more mobile home than house, because the sprout of it was an Airstream travel trailer with silver rust-retardant slapped over crazed metal. It had been built around and onto as labor and supplies permitted, as absolute necessity arose— somebody at the monthly business meeting might notice and bring it up, then later at church workings regret having opened his mouth.

Before the screened porch on the front had been leaned to, the children had slept in the little box bed with Brother Leroy and Sister Mary, wheezing and sneezing, allergic to even their own parents, it seemed, whose prayers throughout the long nights must have given off a warm and static incense like their sleep-softened bedding.

At first, Cliffie had begrudged going there to wait on Sister Mary and the boys while Brother Leroy was away. The raw winter wind whipped and wheeled in the clearing; the tall pines, surrounding, created a sound of rushing; the church itself desolate, godless, empty.

Standing on the porch, ducking low to keep from bumping her head on the plywood ceiling, she would look out over the patch of pewter-green collards at the church and shiver. For all the fervency at services, the amens and vigorous singing, God seemed absent. That's what Cliffie often thought, especially in winter, especially after having been stuck in the flatwoods clearing with the mute, sickly preacher's brood. Before Roy Harris.

Then she would clean the tiny brittle stove, whisk the broom across the peeling tiles, sending their righteous dust flying, and put the pure children down for naps on the jalousied porch. And she would head for the woods behind the church—one more time, always one more time—meeting Roy Harris halfway between Aunt Teat's shack and the church.

Their meetings had never been romantic, so Cliffie would have to invent stuff to keep going. She'd read just enough of her sister Mary Helen's *True Confessions*—every issue saved in a stack under their bed—to make a comparison. Roy Harris was rough and demanding, Cliffie withholding as long as she dared to keep him interested, though not too long for fear he might give up and go back to his old girlfriend, Emmacee Mae, whom Cliffie had never discovered the equal of in those stories. Cliffie had found long ago that she had to block Emmacee from her mind or forget Roy Harris altogether. She couldn't stand to compare or connect him with batty Emmacee. Though everyone joked and called her silly, Cliffie knew she was crazy. During church services, she would fan fast, her white face a blur behind the fan, talking and mocking the amening men. She was definitely abnormal, almost albino, and it pained Cliffie no end to have to equate herself with Emmacee, the scourge of the church. She'd never even been to school. For Cliffie, that alone testified to the fact that

Emmacee was crazy instead of carefree, as Roy Harris claimed. Fun-loving, willing to try stuff.

"Like this," he had said on that first cold day, locking his arms around Cliffie's neck and thrusting his tarry tongue down her throat.

She felt the first tingling of pleasure, then waves of disgust, sitting, jarred by the whole new experience, on a mat of pine straw. Looking off through the thicket of pines that sheltered them from the wind, insulated by their soughing, she was tempted to wipe his tobaccoey kiss from her lips, already chapped. Then Pappy Ocain's dare popped to mind. She took it.

Her heart quickened, raced, and stilled itself by that sheer daring she never knew was inside, the same daring that helped her make it through the ultimate act, which he defined by a dirty word and she termed love: daring herself to complete surrender, love, rearranging what was actually happening until it fit snugly into the print of Mary Helen's *True Confessions*. It took a while.

"Well," he said, arms propped on his knees, and looked off as he chewed on a pine straw, "we ain't getting nowheres." He sighed, got up and brushed the seat of his butt-tight dungarees.

"Roy Harris," Cliffie said, rising to her knees, "come back and set down."

He plopped beside her, staring stubbornly between his knees. A gust of wind above showered them with pine needles. A single russet straw stuck up in his black hair. She plucked the straw, hand passing along his back. "I just wanted us to get close first," she said, concentrating on the long, strained muscles beneath his shirt.

"Well, sug, I just ain't the type to be messing around with no tease." He came out of his pout, brown eyes cutting to her quick.

"I'm not . . ."

"What the hell you call it then?"

Her heart raced; she stilled it, though his ultimatum echoed on the wind in the treetops. "I'm just too . . . ," she began.

"Too good for me, Aunt Teat's foster baby!" He stood and kicked a drift of pine straw.

It covered her foot and she looked down, thinking he was hardly a baby and could leave when he liked, but said only, "No, no," so meekly she hardly recognized her own voice. She hugged his knees, felt him give, kneel, and crumple on top of her.

Fumbling with her skirt—her legs laid open and shivering—he bunched it at her waist and poked at that secret place she'd always thought of as her own until her wedding night, a spot saved, like some valuable, though not-so-rare trinket, for someone she'd love who was ordained by God before she was born, now plundered and spoiled.

As he rammed into her, leering and grunting foul words, his eyes rolled up powerlessly, and she thought of her own power over him and was glad to have sacrificed her virginity for that power. Now, he would never leave her. They were sealed, call it whatever. She gazed up at the sun-sparked pines and stayed with their soughing through the pain, excruciating, electrifying, done.

But it wasn't done.

She still had to traipse back through the cold, singing woods, with her dress matted to her thighs, and face the preacher and then Pappy Ocain.

That was the worst of it.

She had done something she shouldn't have—something nasty (she found she had to keep redefining things as she went) and yet important, because it separated her from them all, especially her sisters in their old-fashioned clothes. And though Cliffie seldom got anything new either, at least she knew how to wear clothes—little things that made a difference, such as pushing up the sleeves of her sweaters. None of them got new clothes, except Mary Helen, who would claw and cheat for a cheap dress from the Smart and Thrifty in Valdosta (Cliffie could glory in the fact that Maude hadn't given in to Mary Helen and ordered her those black ballerina shoes from Sears yet).

Because of their religion, Pappy Ocain wouldn't let them wear dungarees like the other girls at school. Cliffie noticed that he was good at taking a scripture, any scripture, and rearranging the meaning to okay their lack of money and not fitting in at school.

But it was there for the reading, and she'd read it, and besides none of them would dare quibble over possibly another meaning—except Mary Helen.

Coming out of the woods, Cliffie felt different, defiant, picking pine straw and leaves from the sleeves of her white sweater as she slipped into the clearing of the church grounds. Hidden behind a tree, she fluffed her skirt, heart rapping as it did when she used to squat outside Pappy Ocain's bedroom during one of his heart-fluttering spells.

The sun was bright against the white-sand churchyard, where she half expected to see Pappy Ocain waiting for her, fuming with his folded belt. But only Brother Leroy was there, propped on his car in front of the parsonage, hand shielding his eyes in a salute. Wind howling around the church flapped his gray pants legs.

"Cliffie," he said in an edgy voice, "I didn't know where you got off to."

She hugged herself, shivering. "I just went out walking," she said, thinking that trying to fool him was a little like trying to fool God and wondered if Sister Mary was up, sick, cold, and pacing the stuffy house, silent except for the wind buffeting a loose board on one end of the porch.

"Well, I better be getting you on home before Brother Ocain gets to wondering." He laughed.

She knew he suspected something. Her face blazed as she

got into the car that smelled of burnt oil and turnips, vinyl seat cold on her thighs. She thought of several things she ought to say, as he drove along the sun-streaked dirt road, out of the woods. None of them fit.

From the lane, the house looked empty, but black smoke spiraling from the chimney to the cold tin sky was a sign that they were all gathered in Pappy Ocain's room. Cliffie knew she should go straight to her own room, but then she'd probably be under the scrutiny of Mary Helen's curious eyes. Cliffie could usually count on her to be scrunched under quilts in the bed they shared, listening to the radio.

"I shore 'prechate it, Cliffie," said Brother Leroy, "you staying with Mary and the boys." Eyes straight ahead, he parked facing the house (he always had to pump the brakes and pray that he stopped short of the porch).

Two of the liver-and-black pied dogs jumped up on the sides of the car, and their claws raking down metal matched the effect of his words on Cliffie's nerves. She opened the rusted door, said good-bye, and got out.

While he backed the car, weaving among the dogs, she stooped to straighten one of her socks. A rubber band, used to support the worn sock elastic, had snapped and now curled between the folds like a fishing worm. She felt sure that the sagging sock would announce her romp in the pine straw with Roy Harris. Tugging the sock on her prickly calf, she stalled, gazing off at the woods, somber with dusk, at the fields of hazel broom sage, barely rippling and losing light, and the gray dirt yard, a desolate patch, where the dusk seemed to make up from. In winter, the dirt looked like concrete, bumpy gray and clean.

The dogs, bounding back from their chase up the lane, came nosing up to Cliffie, wet tongues lapping at her legs and arms, one jumping up to lick her face. She wiped her cheek on her sweater sleeve and cracked the dog on its cleft skull. It yelped and skulked off to join the others under the edge of the porch, where they all lay eying her from their bed of powdery dirt. Dirt never stirred by rain or wind, but by Kool-aid bottles, tin cans, and loose sills, brickbats tossed at snakes flowing across the tiny funnel pits of ladybugs, or rats scurrying for the dim recesses, nibbling crumbs that sifted through the cracks. Sometimes a child squatted there in the magic of gray, shifting shadows.

Cliffie considered going out back, to the outhouse, but was too tempted by the smoke pluming from the chimney. In the outhouse, she could find privacy, maybe clean herself up; in the house she could get warm. Choices.

Wrapping her arms around herself, she marched up the doorsteps, across the porch, and down the hall, and halted at the door, the last baffle between her and them. She opened it to a blast of racket and heat and milling children.

"I didn't hear you come up." Maude spoke from her chair before the fireplace full of sucking fire.

Pee-Jean scooted across one of the two beds set on each side of the tall room, and dragged a quilt to the floor. Quacker, wedged into the rocker with Maude, coughed like a puppy barking while Maude patiently hulled pecans into the lap of her apron. Each clean brown nut meat was dropped into a fruit jar held between her knees.

In the next rocker, Aunt Teat sat slumped with her elbows on the chair arms. She pressed two pecans together, cracked them, and picked the hulls from the connected nut halves. The fire lit shiny patches on her ancient compressed face.

Cliffie knew that Roy Harris must have been left in charge of Aunt Teat's children or she wouldn't have come. She seldom left them, except for hog killings or pecan shellings, and of course for her weekly begging rounds. Then Tinion Culpepper would drive her in from the flatwoods, being, as Maude said, her closest neighbor with a way to go and good-hearted as they get. Poor old Teat, cooped up in the house all day long with a drove of crippled younguns and that boy too sorry to hit a lick at a snake. But sometimes, Maude would say, it don't look like I can hardly put up with her another minute, poor old Teat.

Aunt Teat mumbled and peered down into her working hands, oversized and rough, as tragic as her wrinkled crone's face.

"What was that, Teat?" Maude spoke up, her flat, freckled face jutting from the bog of Quacker, coughing on one side, and Pee-Jean, rocking on the chair arm. "You got to speak up, Teat, if you want something." Maude settled between the children, the jar of hulled pecans tumbling to the floor. "You younguns would try a saint."

Aunt Teat mumbled again.

Maude ignored her.

Cliffie was surprised to see Mary Helen perched on the scabby concrete hearth, smashing pecans with a hammer, a spreading mish-mash of brown. She glared at Cliffie, bits of chewed pecans stuck to her puffy lips. Her gray eyes roved over Cliffie as she eased closer to the hearth. "You done baby-sitting?" Mary Helen asked, smashing another rolling pecan.

"Yes," Cliffie said, ignoring her in hopes that she would do likewise: Do unto others as you would have them do unto you.

"Don't smash 'em, Mary Helen," Maude said, barely hearable in the racket picking up in the room. The smeary mullioned windows clattered as one of the children crashed to the floor where another had shoved him.

"Y'all cut it out!" Maude said, glancing back, then at Cliffie. "Where's Brother Leroy at?"

"He had to get on home."

"Sister Mary better?" Maude stood and dumped an apronful of hulls on the fire. It blazed and snapped.

"Yes 'um." Cliffie stepped away, then backed as the fire leveled and crackled.

"Them old allergies." Aunt Teat scattered a nest of hulls in her lap, then spat into the fire, between Cliffie and Mary Helen. The rattail streak of snuff on the logs seared and the dry smell spread over the room.

"I ain't never seen you so hush-mouthed," Mary Helen said, sucking on a pecan. She cracked it between her big teeth.

"Sister, bust 'em with the hammer," Maude begged. A dingy pillow flew through the air from the other end of the room and landed at Cliffie's feet. "Y'all quit that now!"

"Them younguns is gone set the house afire," Aunt Teat said, eyes rolling up in her feverish face. "Gone get the upper hand if you don't mind out."

"You younguns find something else to do sides chunk stuff." Maude wrenched around, careful not to dismount Pee-Jean, rocking on the chair arm. Then mumbled, "I might not know much, but I do know my own younguns."

The door flew open and she got up to shut it, wedging into the chair again as she saw that it was only Pappy Ocain coming in. He stopped before the two women with his back to the fire while they studied their laps.

Cliffie could smell cold on him, could feel it in his heavy green coat, as he slid an arm around her. She shivered.

"You ain't cold are you, sugar?" he teased. He took his handkerchief from his hip pocket and blew his nose, a tearing sound.

K.C., Cliffie's younger brother, raised the window over the scaffold, took two sticks of wood and slapped them on the fire. Sparks shot to the backs of Cliffie's legs. She stood still, though her legs burned. The smell of stale coffee grounds rose from the burning oak. She wiped her nose on her sweater sleeve and thought about what she had done and half wished she was little again and standing on the sweeps of Maude's rocker, behind her, while Maude sang "I'll Fly Away" in that needling whang with her head tilting back to touch Cliffie's chin with her soft ginger hair. But deep down Cliffie was glad she had done what she'd done with Roy Harris. Now she had something that none of them could touch and mess up. A secret. She had a secret that didn't pertain to them, like Pappy Ocain's secret of his missing finger. Pearls not to be cast before swine.

But recalling Roy Harris bent over her, that afternoon, fumbling with her panties, she suddenly felt a hot streak of embarrassment. He'd actually looked. An awful leer sharpening his already-sharp features. She had always imagined, when in love, that a couple would kiss and meld without emphasis on the act. Smooth and blending, naturally. It had not been so. He'd not even kissed her while he did it.

Aunt Teat mumbled something.

Pappy Ocain bellowed, godlike, "What you say, Teat?"

"I say they's a sight of meanness out there," she spoke up. "If I was y'all, I'd keep a eye on my girl younguns."

Cliffie saw white.

Aunt Teat stared into the fire, hands going still in her lap.

Pappy Ocain cleared his throat.

"I look out for mine," Maude said. "It's somebody else's needs looking out for." She cracked another pecan, speaking low around the hard thwack. "World ain't no worser now than it's ever been."

Cliffie's face felt as hot as her calves, and she knew it was red. Were they talking in riddles about her and Roy Harris? Regardless, she knew that whatever they had in mind applied only to the oldest girls, herself and, she hoped, Mary Helen, who sat still at Cliffie's feet. The first time she'd ever hoped to be classed with her sister. Close company in tight places.

Still waiting in the truck, Cliffie looked up and saw the circle beneath the black gum break—they're coming—then mend—no they're not. Mary Helen strayed from the tree, hands pocketed in her flared skirt. She gazed off dreamily at the moonlit mist over the woods, then wobbled playfully on the sides of her shoes toward the truck. She stopped halfway and began spinning, skirt twirling and arms out, watching her pinwheel shadow on the ground, while watching Pappy Ocain, who could mistake her play for dancing.

The light in the Sunday-school wing went out. The lights beneath the eaves were extinguished, and moonlight whitewashed the dirt among stamped eyelets of shadows.

Brother Leroy strolled through the side door and kept to the path between the pumphouse and the black gum. As he neared the huddle under the tree, Pappy Ocain called him over. He hung back, laughed, then drew futilely into the shadow. His frail, hunched shoulders rendered a soft drumming sound from Pappy Ocain's patting hand.

Maude lingered dully on the fringe of talk, shifted the baby on her shoulder, and cocked a knee for the biggest baby to clutch. The other children, reining in from the cemetery to the moonlit yard, surrounded her, then pranced about in the lacework of shadows. Rising and falling, their voices were hoarse and worn, fitting for the night.

Cliffie, hearing her name—hearing it clearly in Pappy Ocain's slow, rolling drawl—perked and slid under the steering wheel, holding her breath. A mosquito pierced the mound of flesh on her right forearm. It made her want to grind her teeth. She didn't and she didn't stop the mosquito. Her face grew numb and flushed. She couldn't make out every word Pappy Ocain was saying, but knew the gist of it—his bragging on her. That feeling she hated of having been there before and having heard and seen it all a thousand and one Sundays rushed to her head. Don't do it, Pappy Ocain, she thought, don't do it.

"Cliffie's my favorite—I'll tell the world that," he said. "The rest of 'em ain't fit to kill . . . though Lord knows I love 'em. Cliffie'll make something out of herself, in spite of my hard luck. All things work together for the good . . .

"I'm a good mind to take out that insurance the policy

man told me about, so she can go to college in Valdosta soon as she gets out of school. Ain't but two dollars a month."

"Two dollars," Maude said—always said—"that'll go a long ways toward putting shoes on the littluns' feet come winter. She'll make a way if she's a mind to go." Maude smiled that broken-toothed smile. "Can't do for the one without doing for the others." At times, Maude seemed to rule everybody.

"Yessir," Pappy Ocain droned on, "that Cliffie's gone make something out of herself."

Though inert with listening, Cliffie couldn't hear the rest, but she knew what he was saying—what he always said—and she felt a white-hot implosion in her head.

Brother Leroy nodded, trying to go. Cliffie no longer worried about his telling; now she worried about his listening. Don't brag on me, Pappy Ocain, she felt like screaming, felt she actually *was* screaming through her closed mouth. Don't brag on me. Not to him, not now. She palmed the truck horn, a baleful, ongoing shriek shattering the stillness.

"Y'all come on now," called Mary Helen, coming numbly out of her pinwheel of shadows. "Cliffie's having a hissy fit to get home."

2

J arred from a tunneling sleep, Cliffie spotted Pappy Ocain in her bedroom door.

"Who messed you up, gal?" he said, nothing about him in motion: not his left hand propped on the door jamb, not his feet planted wide apart. His mouth was the mouth of a ventriloquist.

Cliffie blinked against the light, stuttering when she spoke. "What—I don't know wh-what—" She wanted to ask who— who told? when and where? But the words fell apart as fuzz from the whole fabric of her undoing and were after all of little consequence. Pappy Ocain knew.

"You 'bout as well come clean," he said. "Were it Roy Harris Weeks, gal?"

She stalled, hooked on his dead-earnest face, that inevitable question. He would have an answer now. "Go do your talking to Brother Leroy Crosby," she blurted, opting to let the preacher tell, anything to loose the grip of those yellow-spoked eyes. His changing look, from dead-earnest to deadly, warned that Roy Harris had had it.

"Load up on the truck and let's go," he said in a burned-out voice she'd never heard.

She stayed there stiff on the bed; if anyone had yanked the pillow from beneath her head, it would have remained sprung. But she never considered not doing what he said, gripped as she was by those activated eyes. The rumor about his missing trigger finger struck on her mind like a match.

"Load up on the truck and let's go," he said again—a replay in the thick-with-quiet room. Face stone gray, warning ringing on that still, foggy Saturday. House quiet for once.

Where had everybody gone? Since last Sunday night, following her confession to the preacher, Cliffie hadn't had a moment's peace, no time to mull things over. And now her sisters, everybody, had vanished. She could picture them like mice, eyes peeping through chinks in the old walls, where maybe they'd scattered at the first stamp of Pappy Ocain's foot. How had she slept through it all? What was it? How did he find out? Was this a nightmare? The calm, after a week of so much racket, felt like a nightmare. All moments of eventlessness seemed to have mounted up to now, an eventful horror. Her teeth felt sharp, her mind dull, the fog a cushion against energetic tactics.

When she got dressed and out to the truck, backed to the porch and pointed straight into the lane, he was sitting inside with the engine idling, smoke from the tail pipe raveling into the fog that softened the fields and obliterated the woods, the pine tops stamped on the sky, colorless as his face. She hated herself, this place.

He didn't look at her and he didn't speed away—she didn't know what she'd expected. He eased out of the gray dirt yard, shifting gears only once before he got to the barely-hanging gate, the bottom hinge loose and dangling so that you had to pick up and walk it back. She didn't know why they even had a gate.

He got out and flipped the wooden slat, walking it over rank hills of grass. Through the fog the hinges screaked and carried to the truck where Cliffie waited, teeth tight against the racket. She looked back at the house, then ahead at the highway, suddenly wondering after so many years why the

gate had been set midway the lane. Wondering: it was something to do while the hinges screaked, while Pappy Ocain
cursed and kicked, while hating Mary Helen for telling.

It had to have been Mary Helen. Who else? And just as
well her as anybody. Pappy Ocain would have found out
sooner or later, and Cliffie couldn't love her sister less.
Though they slept together, in winter snuggling for warmth,
jointly breathing beneath the covers, they hated each other.
But the least Mary Helen could have done was give Cliffie
warning so she could prepare herself. She handled things better if she had time to rehearse what to say. Otherwise she
stuttered.

Pappy Ocain used to try to make her feel better by saying
that the stutters, like hiccups, were a sign of growing. Then
later one of her teachers at school said stuttering resulted from
a too-large family interrupting what the child was trying to
tell. Well, all of them interrupted, interrupted each other, as
Mary Helen for so long had interrupted her life. And who else
stuttered but Cliffie?

Maude said she made up for it in being "right attractive."
That's what she always said instead of pretty because pretty
meant vanity and vanity was useless—she didn't call it a sin.
And Pappy Ocain would butt in and say Cliffie was pretty as a
picture, modifying the remark to keep on Maude's good
side—not to dispute Maude but to make his point: The spitting image of you, Maude gal, before you wore out a-having
babies and got that tooth broke off.

Maude would cut her eyes at Pappy Ocain and laugh
timidly and coop her top lip over the tooth, one rough hand
flying to her mouth. The light in her eyes would extinguish;
she looked like she was crying. She would look so powerless
then that Cliffie would cringe. And yet somehow Maude had
gained ground on Pappy Ocain with that piece of a tooth.
Some strange sort of power that left him weak and stranded,

and Cliffie would feel weak with him, the broken tooth evidence against him, like the evidence of her small mound of belly, the bad they could do.

Until this morning, she hadn't been able to imagine him mean beyond breaking out a few windows of the courthouse, had only suspected it. But if he was guilty, how could he bring up the tooth, drawing all the children's attention to Maude, who was generally regarded as no more than a sow? Cliffie never joined in because she sensed that the tooth topic was loaded with insinuation, shrouded in mystery, as were so many things about Pappy Ocain: relationships with his children, his kin, his friends. And more: the mystery of Pappy Ocain's past seemed covered, clean sand scattered over his sulfurous ghost.

She examined his gray, strained face while he stamped back to the truck. Then she looked down at the notched stock of the shotgun between them, which jittered with the jittering truck. The door slammed. The gun jerked. She knew what the notches represented, heard Pappy Ocain's eager, rapid breath.

My God! He means to kill Roy Harris. She sat up straight and stared out the window at dewy spider webs tatted from palmettos to pines along the highway. Her lips tingled, her head spun: this was no dream, not even a nightmare. She sat dazed, no closer to knowing, really knowing anything—why she stuttered, whether Pappy Ocain was indeed capable of killing, or what he might do about the baby—no farther away from knowing.

"You had things to do with my girl," Pappy Ocain announced, truck bumper-to-block with the Airstream's doorstep.

Brother Leroy halted at the screen door, then stumbled out the single crumbling step in his white socks, around the two frail children, who appeared to understand intuitively: sensitive, alert to trouble, having been nurtured by the flatwoods and a suspicious congregation. Gently, he nudged the boys back behind the patched screen, like squirrels in a cage. "Why, Brother Ocain, what . . . ?" His apologetic voice cracked. "That Cliffie with you?" He seemed actively pondering how to smooth things over, aware somehow of what things were, yet innocent, his fair hair, absurdly bright, pressed in a cowlick on his febrile forehead.

"Don't you come out here making up to me, boy!" Pappy Ocain said absolutely, prodding Brother Leroy's cocked arm with the barrel of the shotgun.

"What's wrong, honey?" called Sister Mary, gray-meshed and futile behind the screen door. Instantly, she was attuned to what had come round, one more trial and tribulation: that which she'd married him for, not wishing for but taking like a dose of castor oil, a sacrifice to the Lord for her inherent futility.

"Ain't nothing, hon," he said, not looking back, watching Pappy Ocain and Cliffie, the point between, windshield full of mirrored sky and trees. "Y'all want to let's go over yonder to the churchhouse so we can set down and—"

"I ain't got nothing to say I can't say right here in front of God and everybody." Pappy Ocain's jaw locked and he branded the preacher with those yellow-spoked eyes. He spat.

"Pappy . . . ," Cliffie started—she couldn't believe the turn things had taken—and leaned across the seat with an outstretched hand. "Look out for your bad heart." Habit speaking. She didn't know what bad heart meant, could hear her mama's voice in saying it. He ignored her.

"Pappy Ocain?" On her knees now, she crawled across the seat to the open window. "You hear me, Pappy Ocain?" The truck door swung wide, carrying her along, and hit his back. He never flinched; she stayed there at his ear. "Put the gun down, Pappy Ocain."

"See them woods yonder, brother?" he shouted, shattering

the even-morning stillness of the woods, the strained-for-placative tones bonding them all, a circle of silence suppressing his hard-put threats.

In obeisance, Brother Leroy stared off at the woods, where a promontory flat of cleared timber extended: totem poles of leafless cypresses projecting from a plane of crisscrossed pines, the flat, barren and bleached, beckoning. Foreboding.

"You best be seeing can't you make it that far before I have to shoot you down here in front of your old lady and the babies—beg your pardon, Sister Mary." Pappy Ocain used the same tone, strung taut and emphatic.

Brother Leroy blanched, arms limp alongside, tempted to look behind where his mute wife clung to the door, bright in the open and squinting, disbelieving but accepting. Children wrapped in the folds of her skirt.

Cliffie felt her body stretch from seat to outswung door, experienced a blessed brief blurring, then gazed ahead to clearly see Brother Leroy stumble in his white socks across the hacked stubble of palmettos. His socks provided a focal point until she glanced at the raised shotgun, the stump of Pappy Ocain's trigger finger, a tremoring substitute atrophied by fungus. He lowered the gun, cursed—so unlike him—shoved her into the truck, and hopped in.

Slamming the shotgun between them, he started the truck, impatient with its familiar lag and sputter, and cursed again, "Sonofabitch!" The engine caught. He rammed the gear shift against the shotgun, forcing it hard against Cliffie's knee, his eyes riveted on Brother Leroy till he vanished into the woods beyond the cleared plot of trees. "Hot damn!" he said, and Cliffie thought how that was all right in his book because he hadn't used the name of the Lord God in vain.

Losing sight of Brother Leroy, she felt temporarily relieved. Too temporary. Her chest was quivering, eyes hot. Words popped to her mouth, but she was struck dumb. Had Pappy Ocain really taken what she'd said about talking to Brother

Leroy to mean he was the daddy of her baby? It rang in her head, made no sense.

The minute she focused on something—a pine, a scrub oak along a fenceline—it spun away as Pappy Ocain jerked the truck from point to point, maneuvering between stumps, ramming one, charred black, backing up, then off again. "Hot amighty damn!" He added words as his verve stretched.

Watching his excited face, his rejuvenated body, Cliffie thought with a jolt that he couldn't really believe Brother Leroy was the daddy, he was just out to get the first man he came to who could be. Not her fault. Besides, he seemed to have forgotten the object of the chase. It was a hunt, a sport, the who and why nothing now.

Hanging on, she felt hypnotized, their objective lapsing in her mind also, and peered into his stretched, wild eyes, his too-big teeth clamped like the teeth of a steel trap. Why, he was even wearing his false teeth, usually saved for church! Now she knew him, really knew him, as he was before he got saved—his mysterious, before-salvation youth. Such grace in knowing and yet such pain. She felt responsible for his fall from grace. Could you fall from grace?

"Pappy Ocain?" She spoke softly, checking his strutted profile. His hands locked on the steering wheel, turning with it. Those aged, lusterless eyes, irises rimmed an impure milky blue, flicked from tree to tree along the start of woods. Aware that he couldn't hear her, or wouldn't, Cliffie sat back and searched for Brother Leroy, clutching the open window to keep from knocking about.

Soon she spied his white socks picking up and putting down along a hedgerow of myrtle bushes and scrub oaks. She knew Pappy Ocain had spotted him too because he cut sharp and headed that way, the truck bucking over bleached broom sage and saplings. Her teeth rattled. She thought of what he was about to do, that maybe she could stop him, but if she did, Roy Harris would be the one running. Just as well to let

Brother Leroy play decoy—God forgive her—let Pappy Ocain vent his heat. He wouldn't really hurt the preacher he loved like a brother. Besides, this just might work to stall him till Monday—two more days—when she'd be on that bus to Fort Bragg.

The truck stopped before a stand of cypresses, guarding the clearing, and beyond the opening, more woods—tytys, gall-berries, and palmettos nestling pines. A hoop-skirted cypress ahead cast a shadow over Cliffie's side of the truck, warming sun all around.

Breathing harder, he snatched up the shotgun with his right hand, while opening the door with his left, slid out, and closed it without a lapse in motion. The way he closed the door, a whisper and click, reminded Cliffie of how he used to sneak out to hunt deer, Indian-style, leaving her in the truck. He would always come back with a big buck.

She watched him tip off through the brake and disappear into the brushy woods. Listening to the ticking of the engine, the absence of his breathing, the presence of her own, she scooted to the center of the seat to see better.

Above the clearing the sun was dull, moonlike, behind the fog. She stared straight into it, awed that she could, and thought about the time. Judging from the angle of the sun, it was nearer noon than early morning.

"God, don't let him kill Brother Leroy," she said out loud, the hard punch of words fading into the truck's ticking, her sniffling. She could taste the salt of tears, smell her own des-peration, something hot.

Two squirrels spiraled up the cypress ahead, their claws pck pck pck on the stringy bark, and the sound spread to the blue-ing sky, the spot where she watched above the barren flat. Sun rayed through the pines in a diffusion of fog, streaks of light like drifting moon haze. Expecting an explosion, she watched the sun, an irrepressible pressure building in her chest, her ears. Her lips murmured words that made no more sense than speaking in unknown tongues, a grievous outpouring from the heart.

Out of the soundless woods, a crow cawed, flying at a slant over the flat, where barkless pines lay crisscrossed like dried bones. The bird rose to the sun, blue-black wings spread and gliding, and lifted its voice in a raucous cry. At the height of its cawing, the shotgun blasted over the woods, then leveled off to ringing. Cliffie sank. Her heart thudded inside the truck, fog spraying all around, as from the blast, a phenomenon, a veritable end to things. To time. She lowered her head in the melt of sun and shame.

Then she heard both men mumbling over the woods and was reminded that Pappy Ocain's trigger finger was missing. Maybe he had aimed high—though the crow still flew—or maybe Brother Leroy was turning him back on Roy Harris. She should dash from the truck now, find Roy Harris and warn him. But she didn't move; she listened till the voices died and waited for Pappy Ocain to come striding through the clearing. Crossing foot over foot toward the truck, his face was the same stone gray and inscrutable. She expected him to come around to her side and drag her out, maybe whip her.

He got in, turned the key; the starter ground, stalled; he beat the gas pedal with his worn-out foot and the engine fired. Then he backed up, checking over his left shoulder, and drove on through the woods.

Oh, God, she thought, now it's Roy Harris's turn. Squeezing the door handle, she waited till they passed the turnoff to Aunt Teat's, then let go. What did they say to each other out there? What now? She started to itch. She wouldn't scratch and she wouldn't look at him for the rest of the ride home. Was she destined never to know things, destined never to witness endings, only beginnings?

Beside herself, Cliffie kept thinking those words and how she must be. She had heard that old-timey saying so many times.

Either Pappy Ocain or Maude had said that about her last Sunday night when she got mad because Pappy Ocain was bragging on her to Brother Leroy. *She's just beside herself from setting out here so long.* Cliffie never knew precisely what it meant, and hearing it always irritated her. Now she thought she knew.

Sitting at the kitchen table, Saturday midnight, she felt as if she sat beside herself, handholding friends and fighting-mad enemies. One bad, one good. The good one, the hot one, on the left, still couldn't believe the turn things had taken. She hated herself because of Brother Leroy, Pappy Ocain, the whole mess, and felt like rising from the table and slamming open a window, but if she woke Pappy Ocain. . . . Sweat scalded her neck, where strands of hair clung, and trickled to the small of her back, wicking into her white nightgown. The clingy rayon made her itch and she yearned to strip the gown away, but left it to cling in penance for her sin.

"Our Father, who art in Heaven . . . ," she whispered, incapable in her misery of conjuring a prayer from the heart. She stopped, midprayer, got up and raised the window, letting the breeze ride into the room. Glancing out at the starry sky, she unglued the gown and crept to the table again. Prayer dead on her lips. It was too late. She could taste the lie about Brother Leroy—a dirty coating on her tongue. Yes, I lied, she thought, giving herself no quarter as she recalled how she'd told Pappy Ocain to go talk to Brother Leroy—all in the tone. A lie by neglect of truth, a necessary lie to protect Roy Harris. But it was only a three-day lie, not that long. The truth would come out when she was gone.

A sickening effluvium of fried mullet from supper permeated the unpainted walls of the kitchen. The floor sloped to the kerosene stove, reeking of grease and spattered with eggs and cornmeal, grits in shiny patches for roaches to feed on—Maude's scouring bouts had kept merging with mealtimes, till she'd given it up. The rust-streaked refrigerator was buckled in on one side from impact with the backdoor, in constant swing, but like Maude, it never ceased humming, sweating, enduring the pilfering of grubby hands.

The kitchen where they all stayed most of the time, fighting or eating, where Pappy Ocain would get strung out after supper on yarns of olden days. Not really that interesting and mostly repeats—for example, he'd told over and over how Maude, his "Alabama Gal," had traveled with her daddy's sawmill from Alabama to Georgia, how she'd met Ocain and stayed when her daddy moved on (when Pappy Ocain mentioned Maude's having come from someplace else, his thinning skin would glow, as if he were bragging on his wife's accomplishments, what set her apart from the other women in Cornerville). And while the other children would yawn and fidget under the stark overhead light that made the windows bite black, Cliffie would eye her mama, and Maude would smile that broken-toothed smile—thanks for listening. A sleeping baby would be draped, belly down, across her lap, and in the dwindling of Pappy Ocain's drone, Cliffie would drift off to that slow time after supper when she too had slept on Maude's lap.

When had it stopped? When had Cliffie quit being, not the center of Maude's attention, but an aside? As with Pappy Ocain's change, his crossover from lost to saved, Maude's change, her passing from warm to cold, where Cliffie was concerned, could be gauged by a specific event wrought from Cliffie's piddling experience.

Just eight, and already in charge of Maude's new baby, Cliffie had carried her new sister to her mama's bed to change her diaper, and while the infant squirmed with her lardy legs poking through the holes Cliffie'd just fashioned, she had taken Pappy Ocain's can of Prince Albert from the table between his bed and Maude's, taken a cigarette paper and shaken some tobacco to the tissue cuff, rolled it and lit the tip with a match. Scooping up the baby, Cliffie had turned, facing Maude, whose mouth was agape. Cliffie could feel the cigarette bobble between her lips, could taste a grain of tobacco bitter on her tongue, then Maude's hand on her right cheek, the aftersting more radiant than the smack.

Had Maude deduced that if Cliffie could smoke she was grown and on her own, that she no longer needed mamaing? She took a deep breath of air drifting through the window on a murmur of crickets. Dwelling on such couldn't be good for the baby. She surrounded it with her hands as she would a ball, awed and repulsed by the hard mound: it. At first, she couldn't get used to sleeping on her back, but sleeping on her stomach made her too aware of the baby hardening, changing, becoming noticeable. Now she slept on her back and thought about it, feeling the covers weigh heavier there. Alone with the baby, she could almost hear it sigh, as she sighed, hearing throughout the house sounds of them all sleeping, half rousing during the night: somebody mumbling in his sleep or up searching for the slop jar, then snoring around the settling of the house.

She'd always thought of herself as special and separate from them, except for Pappy Ocain, whom she loved so much she couldn't bring herself to dislike him. And the baby was special too, really too fine for Mary Helen to even know about. Now that she knew, Cliffie found it impossible to lie there next to her, obliviously smacking in her sleep. Besides, Cliffie felt sure that Mary Helen had betrayed her.

The floorboards squeaked in Pappy Ocain's bedroom and the sound streaked like lightning through the hall. Sitting straight, Cliffie looked at the doorway and waited, each squeak announcing his coming and letting up as he stepped from rotting sills to sound spots of floor. She hoped maybe it was one of her brothers, who were always up and down, but knew better—she knew every panicky creak of the old house as well as her own body, now fighting back panic of its own.

Pappy Ocain, in dingy, bagging long-johns, stepped to the

doorway, looked in, and shambled on up the hall, body thinning out in the dark.

Stiff, she waited, then heard him peeing off the front porch, his wet tune trailing back. One more day, if they could get through just one more day without somebody getting killed, she'd be on that bus to Fort Bragg.

She would see Roy Harris tomorrow. Sunday. Church. Not that Roy Harris would go to church. He went only when he was scouting for mischief or to please Aunt Teat when he sensed she'd had enough of his stuff and might sic Tinion on him. She was all threat; she never did anything. But Tinion kept a close watch and had warned Roy Harris he'd skin his head if he didn't straighten up and fly right. He'd had it with Roy Harris slinging that curve in front of his house, that souped-up Mercury roaring and swerving ditch to ditch.

That's how Roy Harris had put it, leaving out why he tore up roads in the night. Cliffie knew he hauled moonshine, and he didn't care if she knew; he was proud of his high-speed chases and scrapes with the law. But the last time Tinion got on to him, Roy Harris got so mad he couldn't help telling somebody. Cliffie was handy.

She didn't tell him but she'd already heard the story—or overheard it—from Tinion, with a different slant. She knew Tinion's was more accurate. He'd told Pappy Ocain that he'd had a bait of Roy Harris showing out and worrying Aunt Teat to death and her already with her hands full. The least of it, from what Cliffie could gather, had been Roy Harris racing past Tinion's house and tearing up the roads. Evidently, they'd been at each other for some time. It was there in the grinding silence of the muffled report from Tinion to Pappy Ocain, a straining for control.

Roy Harris gave a different report.

Two weeks ago, he'd perched, slumped, on the long hood of his dusty maroon Mercury, flexing his legs as he glowered off at the woods. "Sonofabitch keeps messing with me, I'll have to fix him." His eyes gave off warning sparks. His hand shook as he dragged on a Camel from the pack laid out on the hood like a picnic between them. Smoke curling from his mouth, he seemed to relax and hopped down to pace along the road.

Cliffie felt like saying that he didn't have to hide his shame with her; she understood, and what she didn't agree with didn't matter. But she noticed that he had backed his car onto the ramp of a logging road, just off the dirt road that ran between his house and Tinion's, one of many ramps leading into the vine-draped woods, well away from Tinion's well-known property line—a fence across a clearing of cow pastures. For all Roy Harris's big talk, that act alone showed his wavering of indifference, even weakness. Cliffie preferred to think of him as vulnerable and needy rather than weak. He was nothing but a poor thrown-away boy needing love. She paced alongside him on the damp dirt road, away from Tinion's property line.

He hooked an arm around her neck, as she tried to match his stride. Her hair was caught, but she didn't dare free it for fear of cutting into their closeness. He needed her, and she needed to be needed by him. She felt light-headed and warm from their eventual blending. Much closer than when they made love.

"I told him it's a free country." Roy Harris spat. "He don't own this goddamn road!" He kicked at the dirt, dun clumps flew, and tightened the arm on her neck. Still rambling, he drew long on the cigarette, then pitched it into the dog fennels off the ditch.

She thought he might cry; she hugged him, felt his fevered body quiver.

"I got connections!" he spat. "If I wanted to have that sonofabitch knocked off, all I gotta do is say the word."

She knew he was scared, a little boy trying to make

points. But, even hating Tinion with him, she also respected the old deacon, wished he could get Roy Harris to settle down—this could be a turning point. Roy Harris's tension scared her, but feeling his bony rib cage, his warm skin through his shirt, she thought how ridiculous that was. He was only talk, and he wouldn't even talk back to a slight, slow-talking man like Tinion.

"He ain't got no right messing in my business!" Roy Harris snapped, and she knew by the way he looked straight ahead he wasn't talking to her. Floating toward them, a fine gray drizzle misted their faces and ticked on the leaves of the bordering woods.

"I love you," she said, saying it as though she loved him even if no one else did. He needed that, needed her. He didn't hear.

Tears welled in his stained eye whites. "I oughta go right now and blow his damned brains out!"

At first, she thought he might, feeling his anger, his almost turning, but she knew he was really afraid. He'd let off steam and let it go. So would Tinion. Their disputes didn't amount to anything. He hated Tinion; Tinion hated him. But neither wanted trouble.

About once a month, Tinion would come bellyaching about Roy Harris, his voice low and inflectionless, on the front porch after supper, and Cliffie would listen for news while Pappy Ocain groaned, raking a hand over his head as he did over discussions of war and depression and Aunt Teat. Poor old Aunt Teat. That's what those discussions were really about, how they always ended: *Poor old Aunt Teat.* Well, what about poor old Roy Harris? He was the one who had to put up with her and that houseful of crazy children.

Though Cliffie hadn't heard all of that last conversation between Pappy Ocain and Tinion, from her crouch in the hall corner, she'd heard enough to know that Pappy Ocain hadn't yet linked her with Roy Harris. Maybe Tinion had and maybe he was hinting at just that and was sparing Pappy Ocain. Or maybe Pappy Ocain knew and was trying to figure out what to do.

Do what you got to, Pappy Ocain had said, voice leaden with restraint. He was sitting in his rocker, feet crossed and propped on the porch post, looking off at the dark-filling yard.

Tinion, leaning close from the other rocker, mumbled in a singsong blend with the crickets, ancient also, preaching and persuading, hand on Pappy Ocain's arm. He didn't mess in no man's business, but that rascal Roy Harris . . .

They didn't understand him. All he wanted was someone to love him the way she did. She could feel the mist, cold on her face. She pulled closer to Roy Harris, face pressed to his chest, and could hear his heart beating. She thought how he suffered, how they didn't understand, didn't practice what they preached: suffering with. *All things work together for the good,* she thought, leaving off the last part, *of those who love the Lord, to them who are called according to his purpose.* She couldn't quite see how the Lord fit into such as this, had to keep her mind on the urgency at hand, which had little to do with heavenly matters and everything to do with earthly matters, the literal ground swelling under her feet, the cold mist on her face, common need. Now he would marry her, and when they got to Fort Bragg, he'd settle down, make a fine soldier, and Pappy Ocain would be proud she'd picked him. He was just young and idle and wild, his bootlegging and cutting up part of that stage. To prove how she felt, she'd let him do what he wanted with her body while the mist ticked in the vines, cold and alert and attuned to the tension rising like vapors from his stiff, hot body. He seemed to forget as he shuddered and closed over her, taking the cold rain on his back.

Pappy Ocain wandered along the hall again, a musty odor preceding his laborious creaking. He stopped at the door, full on, and stared at Cliffie, blinking back the light.

She started to say that she was fixing to go to bed, waited for him to scold, You up all night? Neither of them spoke. His face was leached, almost transparent, fetal head sagging as he ambled off.

She waited for the streaking squawk of his bedroom floor before whispering, "Pappy Ocain, come back," and memorized the hurt in those hollowed-out eyes. Just talk to me, Pappy Ocain, we've always talked. But she didn't really want to talk. If she did she'd have to tell him she'd as good as lied this morning and eliminate Brother Leroy, and then Roy Harris would be as good as dead. Is this how it'll end, Pappy Ocain, close as we've been, me going off with Roy Harris, your last look on my mind?

She still had tomorrow, time to spend with Pappy Ocain, to make things right. But she couldn't undo what was done; no way back, but ahead, ahead with Roy Harris. She would sneak out of church and go to Aunt Teat's house, where Roy Harris would no doubt be left to mind the children for her to go to church.

Nobody ever gave the children's afflictions a name, they were just Aunt Teat's crippled babies. And though Cliffie didn't know their exact ages, she knew they were hardly babies, that the three boys had simply never matured beyond the baby stage. It seemed that ever since she could recall somebody would pass the news around the table with the grits that Aunt Teat had had another baby. Cliffie had been shocked when she learned that Aunt Teat had never married—she'd heard that at school, not at home. What she heard at home about Aunt Teat was usually what she overheard, and precious little of any importance. Cliffie knew that the grown-ups knew where Aunt Teat came from, where the babies came from, but anything linked with Aunt Teat and why she was Aunt Teat was surrounded by pity so thick that where she came from didn't matter. She just *was*, but lots of people in Swanoochee County just *were*—existing, inheritors of each other and each other's persuasions and peculiarities. A bent old woman with three crippled children generated such pity that she ceased somewhere to link to any thing, any time.

But Cliffie could count on Tinion for some scant history: *It's a shame and a disgrace the way John and them boys just dropped Teat from the family. And after her living out yonder in the Okefenoke Swamp all them years, cooking three square meals a day and keeping house for them no-accounts. John's own girl youngun. Called hisself a blacksmith, talked bad to them old crippled-up boys of his'n. Why, one morning, I driv clean out there to get him to fix a piece on my hare, and he got to kicking on the walls of his blacksmithing shop, what hooked onto the house, and cussed them old boys black and blue for sleeping late. Five in the morning. John couldn't get along with nobody.* Tinion would get low, parenthetical. (*Shore good of you, Ocain, to get Teat that Harris old place. Her with them crippled-up babies, another un on the way . . .*)

Cliffie would feel repulsed wondering who'd got Aunt Teat pregnant and how, had even gone through pitying her and the children, so heartrending but removed. It was the longest time before Cliffie even saw them grown—not till she started sneaking over there to see Roy Harris—because Aunt Teat never took them anywhere. She owned one unbelievably small wheel chair, which sat on the porch, seat gathering mildew and wheels corroded with rust. She had no car, caught rides into Cornerville, and couldn't very well trundle them out in the chair to somebody else's backseat, them slavering and grunting over ten miles of rutted roads, another ten of paved, only to get there and bear them in her arms on rounds to beg.

But Aunt Teat had never been ashamed of the children: with each new baby she would cradle him in her short, stout arms, lifting a corner of the faded flannel blanket for anyone to look at the focusless, angular face, a hint of smiling on her tight bluish lips. And anybody dropping by to unload clothes or food would find Aunt Teat just as dispassionately agreeable to inspection as when she went on rounds to beg. Unless they

suggested getting help for the children. Then she would curse
and throw them out, clothes, food, and all, and slam the
cracked front door.

After Cliffie had heard Maude brag about Aunt Teat's ever-
lasting pride at home, she would go to school and listen to
everybody sniggering about old Aunt Teat. The best way to get
back at somebody who'd done you some dirt was to call him
Aunt Teat. If you didn't watch out, somebody might scribble
your name on the blackboard next to hers.

Cliffie didn't make enemies the way Mary Helen did. Her
name would frequently show up on the chalk-dulled blackboard next to Aunt Teat's, that name so common at home, so
alien at school. And Mary Helen would rant and threaten
whoever had written it. She would find out who if it took till
the Rapture! Cliffie would creep along the halls and pretend
not to know either Mary Helen or Aunt Teat, while praying
her idiot sister wouldn't tell that the object of the joke often
stopped by the house. Not that anyone Cliffie cared about ever
came over—none of the girls from school—but what if they
passed and saw Aunt Teat waddling up the doorsteps?

Tinion would drive her into town, to make her usual begging rounds, first stopping off to see Ocain and Maude and
the "littluns."

Cliffie dreaded Aunt Teat's scrunched face, knew she'd
have to bow anyway for the old lady to kiss. (Lately, Aunt
Teat had quit pausing at Cliffie's hall corner, would waddle on
by to kiss the others.) The smell of snuff always ghosted
ahead and behind, like her spirit giving off from her stooped
body. Her waist settled just below her breasts, where a snuff-
streaked handkerchief peeped from the vee of one of two
shirtwaists, both fashioned from the same pattern and pieced
flour-sack prints, pink and yellow patchworks of Robin Hood
in action. Carrying herself in a stealthy, unimpeded manner,
she would cradle her arms under her drooped breasts: timid,
introverted, but always wearing that small smile, face fringed

by thinning gold hair, oddly girlish, splayed at her atrophied nape.

To Cliffie, her young hair and old body made her age as hard to guess as the ages of the children she'd maybe found under toadstools in the woods and now fretted over in the shotgun shanty, floors damp from their slavering. It was all so uncanny: their suffering, that hair, why Pappy Ocain and Maude put up with her.

Waddling, chin down, she peered up from calm blue eyes, mouth hinting at a half-smile, bottom lip managing a dip of snuff. She never said much, but when she spoke, it was garbled, half-sentenced.

"You got to speak up, Aunt Teat." Maude, who never shouted, would shout, kindness seeping around her impatience.

Cliffie had often heard Maude offer to do something with Aunt Teat's hair—a Toni, maybe. And Aunt Teat would almost smile. Pappy Ocain would invite her to stay and eat dinner. And she would almost smile. Then she'd shake her head and slump straight ahead through the open hall to collect Tinion, rocking on the porch.

"You ready, Aunt Teat?" he'd drawl and spit a brown glob of tobacco into the midst of the panicky chickens in the yard.

"'Bout as well," she'd mew and ease out, clutching the guardrail of the doorsteps, with her young hair trying to shine through its need of washing.

"Look out," Tinion would say, keeping idle pace, green twill britches bagging in the seat like an empty satchel. Bald and stocky, green eyes glowing in his tan face, he'd hesitate at the truck, as if likewise confounded by Aunt Teat, his place, where best to grab her for a boost up.

Foot on the fender and heaving, she could never quite hoist herself up. Usually, Tinion would steady her by the elbow, squat and heave, stuff her in, and shut the door fast. Then, relieved, he'd go around the front of the old-but-kept

NECESSARY LIES ■ 49

blue pickup, pat the hood, and get in. And there they'd sit, mum as Sunday, while he patiently worked the key in the switch, listening to the engine putter and fall. When it caught, both their faces would shine—they'd had all faith that it would but were relieved that once again it had.

Out of the goodness of his heart—no relation—Tinion would drive her on her regular route, first, to the post office. Not to get her mail; the post office was just on her round.

As usual stoic, the postmistress, Miss Cleta, flat-faced and white from shunning the sun, would say in a loud voice, "How you, Aunt Teat?"

"'Bout as well as can be expected," Teat would mumble, nod, and shuffle in her holey canvas shoes.

"How 'bout the babies?"

"Same, 'bout the same," Teat would say in that wheeze of a voice, implying that aside from being on the point of perishing they were precious as always. "Thank you, ma'am."

"Y'all keeping warm?" Black eyes fixed on Teat's face, Miss Cleta would reach into a cigar box, pick out some coins, and drop them into Teat's hand, a hint of begrudging in those eyes, in the click of coins passing palms.

"They be beholding." Still and small in the shallow light, Aunt Teat would wait like a child to be sent out.

"Aunt Teat," Miss Cleta would say, "it don't look good, you hanging around here. We got rules to go by, now run on."

Aunt Teat would turn and trudge from the aged white clapboard appendage to the grocery store at the end of the connected shops.

"How you, Aunt Teat?" Hoot Walters would say in a booming voice. Sorting through a hamper of white potatoes, he tossed one into the cardboard box at her feet. "Rotten!" he scolded and straightened up, holding his back. "You don't want that, Aunt Teat!" Conveniently deaf, she continued picking up and brushing off potatoes and dropped them in her pink woven-plastic bag.

"Here." Battling against a sourness settling on his face, he hefted three good potatoes and offered them. "You needing anything else?"

"Just looking." She would browse the four dim, musty rows of shelved staples, canned goods, and enticements tucked between, offset from the produce hampers and checkout counter at the front, where plate glass, each side of the open door, admitted bothered squares of sunlight.

Softly plundering, she might heft a can of evaporated milk, examining first the vague blue price mark, then the picture of a cow on the label, and tuck it beneath the arm crossed on the rise under her bosom. With the hem of her dress, she might polish the dust from a pink plastic baby bottle molded in the shape of a smiling calf, and turning it, stiff-necked, to study the design, set it back on the shelf. And on, feet shuffling, paddle fan whirring above, to a table situated in the middle of the high, dim room with stacked loaves of white bread, sunbeam faces of blond-ringleted girls with pink cheeks.

At the cash register, where Hoot was arranging red and green suckers in a mahogany-trimmed case, she would stoop and peer at him through the glass. He'd peer back, straight-faced, mouth agape, studying. He'd nod and she'd nod, then turn and waddle toward the door.

"Be coming back, heah," Hoot would say, fishing in the candy case. "Aunt Teat, hold up a minute."

She'd halt, waiting as he came around.

"If it ain't too much bother, how 'bout taking them boys some of this here soft candy?"

"They be beholding." She'd turn, entire body, for him to drop four Zero candy bars into her bag on top of the potatoes, canned milk, and bread.

Tinion would be waiting, cross-legged, on the bench outside, facing the morning sun and the biscuit-white, two-story courthouse, across the street at the intersection. "You going on over there, ain't you?" He picked his ground-down teeth with a broom straw.

Hoot would step into the frame of sun and say, "Tinion, make yourself right at home," then close the door.

Aunt Teat would nod and waddle off across the road, again turning whole-body to check for traffic, not once looking at the lone traffic light for permission.

At the entrance to the courthouse, facing the long, dim, hollow hall, she would stand a minute and whiff the dust and old paper and listen to the way-off whirring of a fan, feet shuffling, and typewriters cranking out what would and would not do in Swanoochee County, then begin working left to right, door to door, peeping in and mumbling, "'Bout as well as can be expected."

"How's them boys getting on, Aunt Teat?" the sheriff would call. "Here, how 'bout getting 'em a pretty for me." He'd reach across his desk and stuff a folded bill in the bag clutched to her bosom.

At the tax collector's office, she'd stop and frown, then spit, a glob of rusty spittle sliding down the kick-marked door, and waddle off. But hearing the door open, she'd stop, staring ahead.

"Aunt Teat," the tax collector would call. "I hate to keep after you, but we can't let you stay out there no more if you don't pay up your taxes. Two years we been letting it slide."

Aunt Teat would walk on. "They be beholding," she'd mumble, and shove through the door at the end of the hall.

As Tinion spied her exit through the rear of the courthouse, he'd stand and stretch. Then he'd tug his pants legs and sit again, watching her cross the side road to the one-room brick bank, amble in and out and on to the two-story hotel, taking some time to climb to the top floor and traipse through and out the back.

She'd cross the street and collect Tinion to drive her to the school lunchroom, a couple of blocks east. There she would rummage through the giant aluminum garbage cans stationed on a wood platform.

Miss Ruby, one of the lunchroom ladies, would call out for her to wait a minute. Ducking outside to speak and back into the lunchroom, Miss Ruby would slam the screen door, dispersing smells of warm milk and yeast along the narrow sidewalks on either side of the low red-brick band of class-rooms.

The children on the playground, clustered around teachers in chairs, would quit their games of marbles and tag and holler, "Hey, Aunt Teat, you find erything fitting to eat? You found ery daddy for your babies yet, you old heifer?" Sniggering, they'd scatter out to be reined back by the teacher to their sunny circle of dirt. Aunt Teat would wave and half smile.

The lunchroom door would clap again as Miss Ruby appeared, apron bulging with apples and oranges, government butter and cheese, her wise brown eyes squinting into the eleven o'clock heat, her woven gray and brown hair tucked under a halo of coppery hair netting.

"They be beholding," Teat would say, stretching her market bag for the angel of mercy to dump her apron.

After her rounds, without announcement or apology for having changed her mind, Aunt Teat would stop back by Maude and Ocain's to eat. After dinner, if Ocain was dipping the mangy fice dogs in the fifty-five-gallon drum of burnt motor oil and sulfur, she would stay awhile, kicking around in the dry dirt under the tin-topped shelter.

The squealing dogs would be tossed in brown and white spotted and emerge black and greasy, scampering over the lip of the drum, yelping and shaking. They would dash, gambol, and slide on the warmed gray dirt, flirting dust all the way to the middle of the lane and the long wire gate. They could have bellied under or shot around the posts, where the gaping fence attached, but like livestock, they turned back.

"Heah, boys!" Pappy Ocain would call, and they'd come

running, brushing his khaki pants with oil. "Attaboy," he'd cackle.

Aunt Teat would reach down and scrub one of the dogs between the eyes with a knobby knuckle.

Pappy Ocain would extend his right hand for another dog to jump up to. He'd study the greased yellow dog with hovering, messianic eyes. "Teat, go on and take that ere yeller dog to keep on your yard."

"Couldn't feed him if I had him." She'd keep on scrubbing the dog between its lit yellow eyes as it switched around her faded frock, blackening the hem.

Pappy Ocain's face would cloud over with guilt and pity, with disgust for the dogs groveling round him. "Me and Maude can let you have a couple of dollars."

"They be beholding."

Day done, Tinion would take her back to her shanty in the woods, where the three drooling children slithered like snakes inside the screen door. One might grab her ankle and she'd shake him loose, going on to the grease-dull kitchen with the children wallowing in her wake.

She would call them by name, knowing each self-same, expressionless face—one slightly longer than the others—all pasty-complected, with hazed huckleberry eyes and fine brown hair splayed on their broad bowl foreheads.

When Cliffie went there, she couldn't bear to look at them—who knew but what they might mark the baby?—so she'd keep her back to the door, hear them creep, drop, and slither, feel them breathing through the screen, and smell their pee-steeped clothes.

At the shanty, Aunt Teat would treat her like a stranger, not as she did one of the "littluns" at Ocain's and Maude's. The old woman would shuffle to the door, scowl, and trudge off, her grunting something awful and primal, marked by stern jabs that haunted the house.

3

Cliffie woke the next morning to the chuffing of Maude's pressure cooker in the kitchen before she opened her eyes to a sunspot rocking on her bedroom floor. Leaf shadows from the oak outside her window stirred the dust on that one spot while the cooker matched chuffs with the wind cutting corners around the house.

Ear pressed to the pillow, she listened to her heart, the baby thumping. She squeezed her eyes, breath held in protest of the stewing chicken, her queasiness, Sunday.

Mary Helen, sleeping next to her, smacked and shifted, and Cliffie moved her foot—she'd not touch such a traitor. If she breathed too deeply, she might smell Mary Helen's hair, rank from sweating out the night. Rolling over, she studied the traitor: brown curls tumbled on the pillow, arms flung overhead, showing sheer undersides and pits of grown-out hair, like hog bristles. Her pouty mouth was parted, chuffing with the cooker and the wind. She was sleeping in her blue-striped dress, worn yesterday.

Turning the shame of being judged while sleeping back on herself, Cliffie felt guilty for holding such faults against her sister. But Mary Helen deserved it, she decided, and rolled away to stare at the floor, folding a pillow over one ear, half her face.

While watching the sun shift, highlighting strands of hair,

a bobby pin, a needle, Cliffie thought about Roy Harris. She had to see him today. Her heart hammered away, remembering that tomorrow was Monday and sure as the morning came he'd be waiting for the bus at Hoot Walters's store to travel west with it. Without her, if she didn't come up with something quick.

She sat and felt her stomach, looking at Mary Helen, still dead to the world. Would she take Cliffie's place when she was gone? Would she be as kind to Pappy Ocain when he was foolish? In some ways, Cliffie had to admit, Mary Helen was better—she never slighted her family—a sort of betterness by default. But she could never really take Cliffie's place; Pappy Ocain wouldn't brag on her the same way. Cliffie felt almost sorry for her sister, watching the death curl of her wax-tinted fingers. Pappy Ocain didn't even bother to not show favoritism. But in a way Cliffie envied Mary Helen's not being his favorite, because sometimes Pappy Ocain embarrassed Cliffie and himself and put extra pressure on her to be good.

Like the time Abe Guess, a big-time farmer from across the river, came by to ask Pappy Ocain if the boys wanted work.

Cliffie must have been five then, perception sprouting, standing in the hall, listening, always listening from that claimed corner to Pappy Ocain's untrifled world at the front of the house, as opposed to Maude's busy world out back: the kitchen where a pot of limas steamed, lid clacking, and drifted along the hall; the clothesline full of yesterday's clothes, mildewed sheets tangling with screaming children; the back porch where the rattley wringer washer shook the whole house. Maude's babies bawling.

Peering curiously out at the new green pickup tooling up the lane, Pappy Ocain had strained forward to see who was coming, without moving from his post in the rocker. Reared back with his feet propped, he'd waited for Abe Guess to get out, then said in a high, tight voice, "Get out and come in."

He raked a hand across his head, dipped forward, and spat on the soggy dirt.

"I ain't got but a minute, Ocain," Abe Guess had drawled, swaggering up, lean and alert, with a quality of industriousness new to Cliffie. "I just stopped by to see if one of your boys'd be innerstid in helping me cut my cane."

"Why, I reckon they'd be right obliged you asked 'em." Pappy Ocain's quenched eyes suddenly registered who the stranger was, his high standing in the community, and he plopped both feet to the floor. "Which un you want?"

"What about the one y'all call Cooter?" Abe Guess took off his Ace Fertilizer cap and reset it, tugging the bill low.

"Let me see, now," said Pappy Ocain, glancing back at Cliffie, knowing she'd be there, the go-between, courier, the only one capable, alert enough. "Sugar, run go see if your mommer's had ery hearing from Cooter in the past few days."

She'd dashed off, asked, come back, and told him that her mama said she'd seen him at breakfast but didn't know where he'd got off to.

"Can't keep up with 'em, in and out all hours." Pappy Ocain chuckled. "Them boys!"

Cliffie remembered being aware that he hadn't even seemed embarrassed. At that age she'd thought that, already knowing that Pappy Ocain should be able to give some accounting of his own children, thick as flies on the dogs' backs.

"Git on away from here, sir!" Pappy Ocain hollered at the dogs, yipping around Abe's feet, wet-dog stench heavy as the muddy clouds above. "See that un yonder—that ere dog with the cut ear?"

Abe Guess turned, one slim boot still on the doorstep, and stared long at the moiling dogs.

"That's a German po-lice dog," Pappy Ocain said. Hanging to the porch post, he leaned out. "Cooter drug that un up. Catch anything!"

"That a fact?" Abe Guess watched with Pappy Ocain as the dog waggled off and circled Abe Guess's new pickup, then sniffed a tire and hiked its leg.

Cliffie's face burned. She hated Cooter's dogs. He was always bringing home strays claimed to be pure-bred. If they didn't starve to death, they got hit by cars on the road.

Abe Guess lifted his cap and chuckled, then lumbered off toward his truck. "Looks like it's gone set in raining, don't it?"

"Shore do," said Pappy Ocain, staring at the sagging sky and absently pulling Cliffie to his chair.

Abe Guess stuck one foot in the truck, staring back at Cliffie. "That's a might pretty girl-baby you got there, Ocain."

Lowering her eyes, she shuddered, and put one hand on Pappy Ocain's shoulder. She felt like hunkering away in her corner.

"Ain't she a sight for sore eyes?" Pappy Ocain wrenched around and grinned till his wet gums shone. "Smart as a whip! Done got to where she can just about read, going to school with Ray Lewis ever chance she gets to get broke in for the first grade. Teachers don't know what to make of her."

"That so?" Abe Guess said.

"Yessir, ain't a lazy bone in her body." He squeezed her leg, gums gritted. "Maude can't keep her out of the kitchen— stands in a chair to wash dishes, little bitty thing."

Cliffie's hand pressed hard against his shoulder, signaling him to stop. She didn't mind the bragging as much as Pappy Ocain's saying "sir" to someone younger, someone he considered his better. But she was his and he was hers, so she smiled dutifully at Abe Guess.

Rubbing her sleep-cramped neck, Cliffie slipped out through the hall to the front porch, taking the long way round to the outhouse to keep from going through the kitchen and facing Maude. She hopped off the end of the porch and around the slumped brick chimney, facing Pappy Ocain in the chicken yard.

He was shelling corn, golden kernels trickling from his fingers to the flock of chickens. Their squawking, with the cooker's chuffing, filled her ears as she dodged the chicken yard, tipping along the runner of plum-tree shadows.

Pappy Ocain never looked up. He hadn't said a word to Cliffie since *Load up on the truck and let's go*, yesterday morning. And suddenly she knew why that command had sounded so familiar: that's what he said to the dogs when he took them out riding. When he and Cliffie had got back from Brother Leroy's, the entire house had gone quiet. Now she thought she knew why nothing more had been said. Matters from here on out would probably be handled through the church. It made sense, because if Brother Leroy *hadn't* taken the blame, Roy Harris would be dead by now and Cliffie's legs would be streaked blue from Pappy Ocain's belt that hung in warning from a nail on the kitchen wall. See that belt yonder, he'd say. Y'all let me catch you girls messing around with Roy Harris Weeks and his kind and I'll wear it out on you.

But why *had* Brother Leroy taken the blame? If he had. For all she knew, he could have told. She stepped through the up-and-down board door of the outhouse and eased it to and hooked the latch. Cocooned in the soft brownish light, she peeked through a knothole at Pappy Ocain shelling corn: eyes down, shoulders slumped, brushed by streamers of moss from the dying pecan tree. Corncobs rasping with the locusts. White hens flurrying and scrapping at his feet.

He'd blame the preacher, be put out for a while, might even move their membership back to Cornerville that very day. They'd already made the rounds from Sardis, to Wright's Chapel, across the river, before stopping at the church in the flatwoods. Well, at least she didn't have to worry about her reputation at school. She'd be gone.

Hooked on the hens' clucking, filtering through the gaped boards of the closet, she sniffed the air off the acid-dirt matter of herself and her family. The two-hole bench, sanded smooth by use, looked tempting. She sat, feeling the pulse of air beneath, drained and numb to the outside, except for the images brought in and now scrolling up on the screen of cave-like light with spangles of after-sun: all variations of Brother Leroy's face.

She started flipping through last summer's Sears & Roebuck catalog, 1952, left on the space between the diamond-cut holes, and stopped at the page Mary Helen had marked—a circle around a picture of black ballerina shoes, like her best friend Dottie Jean Belt's. What I wouldn't give for them shoes! Mary Helen would say to her mama, and Maude would say, You got shoes, the littluns ain't; ten dollars would go a long ways toward putting shoes on ever' foot in this house.

Speaking of the devil, Mary Helen now pushed on the out-house door, shook it, blue-striped dress showing through the seams.

"Go away," Cliffie said.

"I gotta be-excused right now." Mary Helen smacked and shifted.

Cliffie could see her bare toes scrunched through the crack of the threshold. "Wait'll I get through."

"What you think we got two holes for?"

"I don't know." Cliffie pressed her feet to the cool earthen floor.

"All right, troublemaker!" Mary Helen warned.

"Just a minute." Cliffie tore the sheet with the ballerina shoes from the catalog, wiped, and limping to the door, bunched her panties about her knees. She flipped the latch and hobbled back to the bench.

Stepping inside, Mary Helen headed for the bench, dropped her dingy blue panties, and settled in next to Cliffie. She still wore her Friday panties. "Friday" was stretched across her rusty knees. She loved those packs of tacky panties, each pair tagged and tinted for a different day of the week: wicked black for Saturday with "Saturday" embroidered in scarlet;

chaste white for Sunday, even the stitching. She ordered them from Sears, resolving each New Year to get her days and panties straight, but she was too lazy to hold fast.

Cliffie listened to Mary Helen panting with the wind, to the chickens cackling, her water beating the dirt.

"What was all that troublemaker business about?" Cliffie asked.

Mary Helen yawned, tapping her mouth. "For me to know and you to find out."

"You need a good whipping ever' morning." Cliffie slammed Mary Helen's arm with the catalog.

"Ouch, you little brat!" Mary Helen rubbed her hard brown arm. "I wouldn't tell you now for all the gold in China."

"For your information, I don't care," said Cliffie. "Pretty soon I won't be around for y'all to pick on, jealousy cat!"

"I ain't jealous of you," Mary Helen said, laughing, "'specially now with your stomach pooching out."

Cliffie sucked in and covered her stomach with her skirt and tallied up Mary Helen's ugliest features, magnified by hot, unspeakable hate: the corners of her mouth drooped, the skin beneath her eyes looked like tarnish, her nose was broad, and her thick teeth were embedded in rolled red gums that showed when she smiled. The best part of leaving would be getting rid of her bedfellow, Cliffie decided.

To get rid of her now, she placed the catalog on her lap and leafed through again. Sliding from between the pages, a letter from Father Flanagan's Boys Town, begging donations, dropped to the dirt at her feet. The white envelope was yellow-ringed and ripped open, where the twins had snitched the stamps. Bending low, she studied the logo in the left corner. A tiny boy with messy hair is riding the back of a big boy. Beneath the sketch, the caption reads, "He ain't heavy, 'cause he's my brother."

Cliffie kicked it at Mary Helen for her to read. Mary Helen

glanced down, sniggered, and kicked the envelope back. Brought out of her daze by Mary Helen's stupid attempt to play—her collapsing that end of the seesawing rift—Cliffie finished her business and stalked out.

Mary Helen shouted through the shut door, "I do feel sorry for Brother Leroy and them."

As Cliffie slunk back toward the house, Pappy Ocain eyed her. She stared down at her squat shadow in the play of plum trees stenciled on the dirt.

"Y'all get fixed up for church now and quit that quoiling." He turned away, his back to Cliffie.

For some reason, his sour mispronunciation of "quarreling" made her feel sad and guilty, so sorry for him. Tears formed, like a melt of iced eyes, and she tried to swallow the sorrow, to go cold again. She could lie to everybody else, but she couldn't lie to herself. She still wanted to leave the old house, hated the tar-papered tobacco barn, ribbed with bark slabs, hated the chicken yard, closed in by a lace of chicken wire tacked to slats rotting at the dirt, hated the poor-dirt fields, fit only for growing broom sage. She hated the sorry dirt of the yard, impressed with footprints and working up bits of glass with every rain, even hated the wild woods that cut them off from the rest of the world. But she did wish she hadn't hurt Pappy Ocain, wished he'd always known her as unworthy of his trust. She'd never been worthy—shouldn't have had to be. Nobody else had been obliged to amount to something.

She watched his slumped back, crossed by the galluses of his bib overalls. The skin on his neck was a waxy tallow shade. That bothered her. She'd grown used to the lobe of his left ear's being cropped, like the German police dog's—no rumor about how that came to be. But now he looked pitiful and whipped. Wisps of pinkish hair stirred at his nape. With languishing eagerness to leave, she watched his right hand shelling corn, as if he never really needed five fingers in the first place.

Crying inside, she felt like ulcers were bleeding, oozing throughout, and tortured herself by keeping the heat of hurt from passing through her tight eyes and lips. She pictured Pappy Ocain, on the dark side of her eyelids, as in a snapshot: defective, suffering, and old. Yes, old. Before, she'd thought of him as only worn, ill, and aging. The recurring fear that he was always on the verge of dying from his bad heart—which she could now see as a withering chicken heart in the snapshots shuffling before her eyes—had somehow eased up with her other early fears, the natural and not-so-natural fears of all children: loss.

She used to sit against the door frame, outside Pappy Ocain's bedroom, during one of his spells, while everybody scrambled and screamed for help. She would always feel spellbound and frozen in the cold and coming dusk, sun slanting across the dusty floor of the hall and illuminating his gasps in a visible audio, a spiking of sound waves before her eyes, frays from his fraying heart rising to the shadowy recess of the ceiling.

She could never bring herself to look back through the open door where he lay gasping and groaning on the bed. She could imagine him white and dying: bone-tight face thrust to the ceiling, chicken neck arched, legs palsied and taut, and his bad heart, so tender and good, at the center of it all, flushing within like a bevy of quail. Her own heart would race with his, and she'd grow chilled and desperate for air. Praying in spangles of the tight near-death ecstasy, Lord have mercy on us all!

The spells came about once a month; Cliffie never learned to predict them, was always surprised, no matter how she lay each night dreading and believing that in predicting a spell tomorrow she might head one off. Then Maude would holler for one of the younguns to run lickety-split to Miss Sula's, down the road, and call Dr. Quacker in Valdosta to come quick. "Your pa's a-dying!" she'd holler out behind Cooter or Roy Acuff or Scooter, scuttling off at a tilt up the lane.

Cliffie, usually quick to act in a crisis, never offered to go. She couldn't move and had that to add to her growing collection of guilts. She would just sit there while the others wailed the same declaration in different arrangements: *He's dying this time. This time he's dying. Time he's dying* this would ring in her head, and he hadn't died yet. But with each attack, Cliffie died a little, strength ebbing till any more would have been too much. And after every attack, she'd be grateful to the Lord that Pappy Ocain hadn't died yet, until finally she hardly noticed Dr. Quacker's plain white car wheeling down the lane.

How she despised that doctor! All silvery gray, round and jolly, silver-rimmed glasses set on his bulb nose. She hated his cheery nonsense, his apparent indifference to Pappy Ocain's dying. He'd stomp into the bedroom, a laugh broke out on his antiseptic face, and shoo everybody away from the bed, except Maude. He'd roll up his white shirt sleeves on giant hairy arms and mold alcohol-soaked hands on each side of Pappy Ocain's throat, bearing down and whooping like a preacher, "I'm gone choke you to life, Pappy Ocain."

Maude, hovering over the bed, would simper.

"Mama Maude," Dr. Quacker would crow, "you better pay attention."

After witnessing the first session, Cliffie refused to watch with the others, all crowded self-consciously in the doorway. She'd hold her breath, controlling death: if Pappy Ocain lived, she would too; if he didn't, neither would she.

Suddenly, he'd pop up with a holler and whoop, everybody tittering, ready to celebrate with a big supper.

Now, Cliffie would think, he'll die. When you least expect something, it comes: her childhood motto. Trying hard to expect everything bad, nothing good, warding off and bringing on. . . . But she would hear Pappy Ocain's heavy brogans smack the floor, shaking the aged house, hear the bed springs squeak—the way he pressed down and feebly stood, trying his legs. He'd brag on the doctor, voice weak and building apologetically, strengthening on the presence of a dignitary in the house. And Cliffie would cringe, praying that when she closed her eyes the doctor would vanish like dust into shadows.

They would all come parading out, Pappy Ocain feebly leading, like Lazarus come from the dead, the doctor marshaling everybody along the hall to the kitchen, where they'd pay for the miracle with a supper of fried ham, hot biscuits, and cane syrup. A bottle to go.

The doctor's real name was Dr. Coppage, but everybody had trouble getting the name out quick and started calling him "Dr. Quacker"—even named one of the twins "Quacker" after him—after Cliffie had called him a quack. To his face. On that first visit. He didn't mind, he roared, long as they called him. His booming laugh-and-talk reverberated from the kitchen to the hall, where Cliffie stayed whenever he came from that day on.

"You got a fine bunch of younguns, Ocain," he'd say, "and a good-looking wife to boot."

Maude would giggle and blush, switching on that something never used within her.

"Where's Cliffie?" Pappy Ocain would say.

"Which one's Cliffie?" Doc Quacker would be struck dumb, as if absolutely amazed by the multiplying faces. Could there be one more, one called Cliffie?

"You ain't never seen a prettier girl-baby in all your born days, Doc," Pappy Ocain would boast. "Cliffie, get in here."

Cliffie would stay scrunched beside the bedroom door in the dark hall, waiting, waiting for Pappy Ocain to come back and collapse on the bed. She wished they'd quit feeding the doctor who choked Pappy Ocain, who even encouraged meek Maude to choke him. Couldn't they see he made fun of them because they were poor and quaint and fools?

"Cliffie, run try on the frock your mommer just made and show off for the doc!"

"She's sulling."

"How come?"

They would all laugh, sounds spilling from the lit doorway of the kitchen and stopping in the light at her feet. She would feel ashamed of feeling ashamed, and of her fear of Pappy Ocain's coming relapse, of her failure in prediction.

Why did that quack choke Pappy Ocain? Why did they play up to him? Hearing Roy Acuff tuning his guitar for a recital, humming in a high falsetto—that derned doctor laughing his head off and her sisters squealing as he yanked their plaits—Cliffie lowered her head to her knees. Why did Pappy Ocain, with lazy resignation, rise and go back to sit on the front porch, telling everybody who came by about the episode till the next episode came? He'd tell them over and over about "the doc" eating with them, "just like one of us."

"How bad is his bad heart?" Cliffie had asked Maude one morning.

"Bad," she said, staring through the kitchen window at the sun mirrored on the corncrib tin.

Cliffie had stood there, satisfied while her mama stayed and parted the curtains on the window, satisfied while the morning stayed, peering in as Maude peered out. Something mellow growing from the dawn, preceded by the grip of night.

"Will he die?" Cliffie asked, touching the soft cotton of Maude's skirt.

"Hum," Maude said, eyes languishing in the light shifting on tin, her hand stiffly stroking Cliffie's hair. "Run go play."

Cliffie knew that Maude's "hum" and "run go play" meant

yes. So she'd gone outside to play, knowing, always knowing and keeping it inside until finally, from lack of proof, the fear languished.

Cliffie had about concluded that Pappy Ocain was only old: a holding, stagnant state. She had no idea how old he was, maybe seventy, seventy-five. He looked older, shelling corn like a wax statue with movable hands. Even if he was only seventy, in ten years he'd be eighty, and Cliffie could recall no one she knew of having lived much beyond eighty. How could she leave him? How could she stay? Would her staying kill him quicker than her going? What if she never saw him again?

She could tell that he knew she was there, wistfully pondering him, the situation, that he was thinking about her too, that he loved her more than anyone else in the world, that he needed her, though she never ran to call the doctor or stood over his bed during his heart spells. Without her posted outside the door, he would never have pulled through. He could trust her tears to mark the door, like Passover blood, so that the Angel of Death would pass him by.

"Pappy Ocain," she said, feeling the wind on her back like the Holy Ghost.

"You busting to say something?" He half turned toward her. He would give her her say. One chance.

"Get out of the way, prissy pants." Mary Helen shoved past, mincing along the path of plum-tree shadows toward the house.

Pappy Ocain started shelling corn again, squinting at the sunny slants on the chicken yard. A locust joined the chic-chic chickering of a black bird with an orange gorget.

Cliffie would write to him when she got to Fort Bragg; she might write to everybody. Except Mary Helen. She wouldn't even speak to her when she and Roy Harris came back home to show off the new baby—maybe a girl (Pappy Ocain would like that). She would write to Brother Leroy too, who she knew would be judged and sentenced tonight. Nothing would happen at church this morning; any business to come before the church was always conducted after the night service at a special called meeting. Regular morning services were never disrupted: Remember the Sabbath day to keep it holy. Night was okay. The calm now, set off by the hissing pressure cooker, the wind, and the locusts, announced something was up. No other explanation for this Sunday-morning lull, this brief muttering brink-of-things.

Sunday sunlight seemed to Cliffie always thinner and brighter, the sky a bluish-yellow cast, sharply defining objects, faces. A slow time, elastic and light.

Standing before the desilvering mirror of the mahogany dresser in her bedroom—alone at last—Cliffie brushed her thick blond hair into a ponytail. Roy Harris loved her hair that way, especially with a ribbon tied in a bow for him to yank. Fisting the ponytail, she plundered in a dresser drawer with the other hand, uncovering Mary Helen's pink satin ribbon, lipstick-smudged and frayed. She untangled it, sure it would be long enough, even with the ends snipped at clean angles. In a search for scissors, she tumbled face powder, rosy perfume, tubes of lipstick, and bottles of nail polish in thickening exotic colors, while watching the open door for Mary Helen. If Cliffie could manage to tie the bow and make it to the kitchen before Mary Helen came in to dress for church, she wouldn't dare snatch the ribbon.

Cliffie could hear her muttering out in the kitchen. Her voice always sounded as if her tongue pulled against gooey spit on the roof of her mouth. Usually she talked loud, but this morning Cliffie couldn't make out a word.

All rooms opened into the hall, leading from the front porch to one end of the kitchen at the rear. None of the wainscoting had ever been painted, but all of the children had contributed, in spurts of creativity, to decorating the hall: an orange crayon mark unraveled along the silvery brown wall, from the front to the back-porch water shelf, looped and stopped at the reddish heart-pine frame of the entrance.

Roy Acuff, next to the oldest, had left his name in double-traced pencil: "Roy Acuff was here." He'd written it on a Saturday night, right after quitting school. All the boys quit as soon as it was legal. They were always referred to as "the boys," and everybody would always say, Say what you want to, but Ocain's raised some fine boys, which meant they kept to themselves and stayed out of trouble. And Cliffie, learning that quitting school was legal at sixteen, gauged each of their ages by when they'd quit.

She had witnessed Roy Acuff's turning on that moonlit summer night as in a dream: the hillbilly whang of the "Grand Ole Opry" on the radio skipping fuzzy down the hall and through the open door (in summer they never closed the doors to the hall; chose to put up with mosquitoes in a swap for air). Music filtering into her sleep, she'd heard his knuckles rapping on the kitchen table, his feet drubbing on the floor. Then weaving in and out of sleep, she'd heard his flat feet slapping along the hall and spied him writing his name on the wall. Head raised from the pillow, she could make out his eyes, ghastly with a glint of dreaminess, his hands writing, as though putting down who he was would make it half-so. Moonlight making the night stretch, and with it the dream.

Cliffie, loving color—always begging Pappy Ocain to paint—now thought how she'd hate to see Roy Acuff's silvery, sometime-detectable name painted over, like a cobweb raked down.

Next to his name, someone had hung a bow, crafted of tobacco twine, from one of a blue-dozen nails hammered into the hall walls. Things shifted from nail to nail, according to season, use, imagination: coats, hats, a coil of hay wire. An orange construction-paper picture of a stick man now hung on one of the nails, punched through his head. One of the twins had drawn the picture in first grade, the year before, and it was beginning to curl at the corners, flapped and scraped with every breeze. And invariably somebody at the supper table would ask, What's that? and Cliffie would invariably remind them. They never remembered; they never really thought about anything, just sounded off, responding from the senses like a pack of dogs.

Despite Maude's mild scolding, they all would crowd around the table and cram, down to the last bean, burping and unruly. Believe I'll have me a mouthful of them grits, Pappy Ocain would say, poking his plate from the end to the center of the table, over pots of food where spoons clanked from a dozen hands. Corn bread, sidemeat, and sweet potatoes grabbed in a flurry, everybody shoving, shouting, burping. Say excuse me, Maude would say weakly, forgetting it as somebody knocked over a glass of iced tea and syrupy rivulets ran the length of the table, around pots, trickling off the oil-cloth to laps. Then they would fight over whose fault it was and who had to clean up the mess. Maude always did it. She'd dab beneath the pots and plates, then drop to her knees and mop the floor while everybody ate.

After supper, the older children would wash the dishes in the mended dishpans so Maude could "lay down with her bad back." During those spells, she would lie listlessly, barely able to whisper, summer-cold soot strong in the fireplace, shadows tomwalker tall on the walls, voices chiming in from the kitchen, baleful, lost.

They would grumble over pans of greasy dishwater, fearing that they could be taking on all of Maude's duties for who knew how long, unable to even imagine what those duties involved. Then, taking advantage of Maude's being down in the back, they'd sling wet dishrags at one another, knowing she couldn't get up and switch them with the tea weed kept behind the door. A chair might overturn, crashing to the floor, and a fight would break out. Once, Cliffie played dead to make Mary Helen quit socking her.

"You younguns is gone be the death of your mommer," Pappy Ocain would say from the kitchen door, grazing all with pitiful eyes. Then he'd go back and pace the hall, waiting for Maude to get up and take charge.

His saying that always got a response. Grumbling lower, they would finish the dishes, sweep the floor, and mind the babies.

Going out into the whispery night to feed the dogs, Cliffie would think about how like the dogs her sisters and brothers were, dogs yapping and snarling around her feet as the children did Maude's, for the pot of table scraps. Cliffie would have two children, a boy and a girl. No more than three. She tried to think who might have been weeded out of the family to bring about some order, and decided Mary Helen, then felt guilty, recalling how Mary Helen had boasted, I take up for my family, after a run-in at school that day between a bully and one of the twins. Cliffie always avoided them all away from home.

In the mirror lit by Sunday sun, Cliffie powdered her face from Mary Helen's Angel Face compact. Limping steps along the hall caught her attention, and pivoting the mirror, she spied K.C. loping past her door. His right foot was bound in a white strip of bedsheeting. Cliffie recalled someone's saying that he'd gotten a splinter while scaling the brace of a fence post. All last week, she'd felt hard of hearing, now her ears picked up every sound, and there was nothing but chuffing and muttering, birds tweeting softly.

A chair in the kitchen scraped across the floor, and Cliffie suddenly realized that all of them had gathered for breakfast without once shouting for her to come on, without once shouting anything. Secretive, worrying, the ghost of their unique silence wandered along the hall. She was being treated as an outsider. Who had spoken to her this morning? No one really, except Mary Helen, who didn't count.

After Cliffie and Pappy Ocain had come back from Brother Leroy's yesterday afternoon, she'd kept to her room, locking the others out. Flipping the tiny lever on the square metal lock, she'd turned the porcelain knob, testing the lock, and found it worked for once, then lay numbly, face down on the bed.

At some point she had got up, sun playing tricks with the shadows, and unlocked the door before anybody could bang on it or rattle the knob, and lay down again, drifting off to sleep because being awake and aware took too much effort. Later, surrounded by the leveling dark, she woke to her sisters sleeping and eased out.

Aware, now, that the racket of the pressure cooker was muting their toned-down talk, Cliffie dreaded going into the kitchen to face them. Even the buzz of the locusts squelched them—such a sad tone to the combination of running murmurs. Why, her family was actually behaving like other people, for a change! But realizing that she was the reason behind all that quiet, her heart sank. She had to go in there; things had to progress in an ordinary-Sunday fashion so she could make it to church.

The hot draft in the hall ruffled her ponytail, and walking on she pressed both hands to her face—it would be so easy to go back to her room, to play sick. But she had to see Roy Harris. As she stepped through the kitchen door, the inflated hiss of the cooker, and the deliberate hush in the round of lifted faces, made her ears feel like they needed to pop.

Maude sat in a chair, facing the brown high chair decorated with a decal of a fading teddy bear. The baby leaned toward her and opened her pink moist mouth. Maude smacked and sampled the buttery mixture of grits-and-eggs, saying, "Ummmm," then touched the spoon to the baby's lips. She turned her head. Studying the baby's yellow smeared face, Maude tipped the spoon and craned her flat, freckled face, tempting the baby to eat. She tasted and let it dribble down her forming chin. Maude caught the dribble of spit and grits and spooned it back into the baby's mouth. She sputtered.

"You don't eat it, Pee-Jean will," Maude said sweetly, clicking her tongue. "One more." And started over.

"There's Cliffie, Mama," said Quacker, one of the twins, gnawing on a finger. She overturned a glass of milk as she pointed at Cliffie, her blue eyes darting beneath spun-glass bangs, freshly cut (Mary Helen was forever whacking on their hair).

"Shut up, Quacker!" said Pee-Jean, Quacker's carbon copy.

"Y'all go on and get done eating." Mary Helen wiped the milk from the table, grazing Cliffie's shoulder on the way to the dishpan.

Maude, looking at the baby to keep from looking at Cliffie, sat hunchbacked in her latest whipped-up dress: a brown shirtwaist of Dan River plaid, left over from the fall line of Hoot Walters's piece goods. Hastily cut and stitched on the treadle sewing machine, the dress showed basting threads, puckered seams, and tight-bound buttonholes. "You ready to get down?" she whispered to the baby. There was always that intimacy with each baby, gradually diminishing as the child got older. Maude unlatched the high-chair tray and caught the tilting baby in her wet, droopy diaper.

"Let me go get Squirt ready for church." Mary Helen strutted over, adjusting the waist of her red poplin skirt. She wore a white eyelet blouse, dirty bra peeking through the eyes.

Maude passed the baby to her; the baby whimpered, reared, and gave over to giggling as Mary Helen sputtered on her blown tummy.

Maude looked at Cliffie for the first time since her condition had been translated to fact. Cliffie thought about how the last time her mama had looked she'd been innocent and pure in Maude's eyes, how sudden the shift to being a hussy now that Maude knew, how time and circumstances play tricks, while really all along . . .

"Breakfast is on the stove," Maude said.

"Thank you, ma'am," said Cliffie. "I ain't all that hungry."

"Eat you some breakfast." Maude's eyes locked with Cliffie's.

Cliffie winced. "Yes 'um," she said, thinking, Is this your only reaction to me having a baby? Placing me in the same category with you, baby-maker?

Cliffie felt foolish, like she was playing at being grown-up. Irreversibly adult. She'd done it now. She couldn't go back to being that typical teen, the image she'd tried so hard to project. Her ultimate dread had always been to wind up like her mama. She took the last biscuit from the platter on the stove, while watching the shuffling round cap on the pressure-cooker lid, chicken steam rising white to her face.

The chuffing of the cooker had become such a part of the morning backdrop she hardly heard it now. The chicken hardly sickened her. Her family hardly bothered her now—probably in psychological preparation for leaving, Seventeen magazine would say. She might never see them again, nor the greasy kitchen, the bulking veneer of the backdoor, propped open with a jug of greenish-brown cane syrup.

Aware of Pee-Jean and Quacker still behind her at the table, she sucked in and smoothed the front of her pink sundress. She nibbled the biscuit, sogging in the steam of the cooker, and couldn't hear whether Maude had left the room. Had Pappy Ocain come in? Were they all studying her for some sign? She felt rotten. Regardless of how poor they were, no one in the family had brought real shame on the Flowers name. And, ironically, she'd been the one expected to bring honor to the family—the first Flowers ever who would graduate from high school, Pappy Ocain always said. She thought how respected they would be now, minus her, poor but honest white trash.

Tears formed with the steam in her eyes, a mesmerizing blur. Roy Harris will marry me now, she thought, no matter how he feels. She'd make him, had needed all this time to get to boiling point. She almost hated him, but knew she wouldn't show it when she saw him. She was glad for the push, but still knew he'd not be driven to anything; she had to lead him. She sucked in, turned, and marched out. When she got to Fort Bragg, she'd set everything right. Then Pappy Ocain could brag about her going to Fort Bragg.

Keeping that saying in the back of her mind, *brag about going to Fort Bragg,* she made it to Sunday school, ten long miles with the wind swaying the truck, wigglesome children heaped on top. The oldest always formed the bottom tier. That arrangement put Cliffie in direct eye contact with Mary Helen, in the middle, after her neck had begun to crick from straight gazing out the window. She couldn't keep breathing into Pee-Jean's sour dress.

"Tie Pee-Jean's sash, will you?" Maude, next to Pappy Ocain, said to Mary Helen.

"I would if I was over there," Mary Helen said, smacking at Cliffie.

Brag about going to Fort Bragg, Cliffie said to herself, smiled, and tied the blue cotton sash in an exaggerated bow, then pressed the creases with her fingers.

"I'd smile if I was you!" Mary Helen said.

"Mary Helen," Maude said, in a fizzling attempt to muzzle her.

Cliffie covered her nose and mouth with her hand to keep from smelling Mary Helen's breath, which she hadn't actually smelled yet. But she made her point.

Mary Helen yawned, suspiring. Pee-Jean ground her bony rump into Cliffie's lap.

"Set still, Pee-Jean," Cliffie said, handling her tiny waist, hoping her own dress wasn't rumpling too badly, that she wouldn't smell like dried pee when she got to church. (Maude had nicknamed Jean "Pee-Jean" to break her from wetting the bed—it hadn't worked yet.)

As Pappy Ocain slowed to turn off the highway to the dirt road leading to the church, he cleared his throat and spat a wad of yellow phlegm out the window. Myrtle bushes and sweet gums flailed the pickup as it jostled over ruts. The last rain had gullied the road, and sand had washed to anthill-like beds in the scummy ditches. Divided by a green weed middle, the double paths glared in strips of sun. Tall pines flanked the road and spread west to the Okefenokee Swamp, acres of palmettos, gallberries, and gators.

Mary Helen shifted, trying to scoot Cliffie with her hip.

Cliffie smiled and clenched her teeth. *Brag about going to Fort Bragg,* she thought, the rhythm and truth and absurdity of the thought her only salvation in the cramped truck. Bars of sun and shade, rolling over the truck, made it feel like a jail.

What if Roy Harris absolutely refused to take her? She couldn't quite fathom what next if he did. Would she end up like Maude, scrunched beneath a brood of her own nicknamed, cross children, off to the same dull church every dull Sunday, the whole week revolving around that one destination, starting over on Monday? Could Cliffie be content, as Maude seemed to be, with staying in Swanoochee County the rest of her life, breeding and dying? She doubted it. Gazing at Maude's raddled face, Cliffie couldn't imagine ever becoming so old and stale and out-of-step, so wretched with duty and doing.

She thought about Maude's single attempt to assert herself, a couple of years ago, when she'd bought a Holy Bible from a traveling salesman.

Salesmen were always stopping by, as though suckers could be identified by their ramshackle houses and their distance from the highway.

The Watkins man stopped by regularly, and Pappy Ocain

had been suckered into buying a bottle of Watkins liniment after the old man swung his rangy leg over the hood of his Studebaker to demonstrate the oil's regenerative powers. In addition to the bottle of sharp, yellow rubbing oil, Pappy Ocain had bought a box of rat bait, which stayed on the shelf in the pantry, where the rats got into the rice and flour sacks.

A vacuum-cleaner salesman came by once and enlisted the children to help sow dirt like seed peas on Maude's just-scrubbed floors. He'd vacuumed the entire house before naming the price, even vacuumed all the mattresses to demonstrate how their skin shed in the night. They couldn't afford the machine. Were disappointed.

An encyclopedia salesman once brought samples of fine-print books about places and events that didn't pertain to the Flowerses, their drab locale, and what they needed to know to survive. Along with the books, he brought proof of the children's bad grades, pilfered from school records, but under the threatening glares of the children he made a dash for the door without the sale. "Them younguns ain't brung home no report cards like that," Pappy Ocain had said of the copied reports. They never did bring home report cards; they always signed them for Ocain and Maude. Maude said, "Hum," going off to the kitchen.

But when the Bible salesman dropped by, Maude came out of the kitchen and switched on that something seldom used within her.

The mild young man bowed over his order pad, scribbling, while Mary Helen flirted and the other children plundered in his black satchel, bulging with Bible-story books and Bibles.

"That's one thing I'm gone have myself," Maude said to Pappy Ocain and pointed to the large brown Holy Bible, embossed with gold and illegible rubrics. "My younguns is gone have names for theirselfs, put down in the Bible."

Pappy Ocain had started to protest.

"This ain't *Teat!*" she'd spouted before he could say a word.

Then he stomped off to his end of the porch while she dragged up a rocker on the other end. She sat almost leisurely, fidgeting and rocking, stout legs properly crossed. She kept smoothing her faded frock, as if she didn't want to act too eager or too proper, being plain and poor as she was. She bought the Bible anyway. And no one had challenged her. They were amazed, proud—especially Cliffie—because Maude had finally asserted herself, but having done so, she soon shrank back into her kitchen.

Cliffie had watched Pappy Ocain, whittling on the porch post on his end, and wondered what he'd say to Maude about her one extravagance after the salesman left. And what had that remark about Teat meant? Nobody else seemed to notice that Maude's remark had carried more force with Pappy Ocain than the broken tooth ever had. He looked like a man who had changed—before the transformation as sinful as he was now saintly. He sat quiet and inscrutable, while Maude placed the order for the Bible. That had to have been close to his turning point, Cliffie decided, estimating by testing expressions between Ocain and Maude.

As soon as the package came in at the post office, one of the children had carried it home to Maude, and they'd all gathered round the kitchen table on the long benches to watch her rip tape and wrapping away. She'd sat at the head of the table, in Pappy Ocain's chair, and carefully printed each of her children's names and birthdates, to the best of her recollection, head bowed over the gold-ruled lines, while an embellished Jesus in the Garden of Gethsemane gazed from the corner of the green page. Gold-gray head bobbing and eyes alight, she would pause to concentrate because the ink wouldn't erase. Once she tried, but gave it up, tracing over Cooter's name.

Cliffie had felt proud to witness Maude's careful entries—each child special, separate, irreplaceable. Always before she'd felt like a member of the masses, noisy, indistinct, contributing to the hubbub. But she'd felt strong, with Maude strong—Maude taking over and seeing to the proper family recording in the Bible so new and smelling of ink.

At the church clearing, the truck dipped into a washout, jolting everybody, and they all squealed—except Cliffie—as on a roller-coaster ride.

"Y'all act right now," Maude said weakly, what Pappy Ocain usually said on Sunday mornings.

And Cliffie, taking note, thought about how Maude was speaking and acting for him till he could get a grip on himself. It'll all come out in the wash, Maude had probably said to Pappy Ocain about Cliffie's predicament. And it infuriated Cliffie because the remark ascribed to her own life the ordinary, though extraordinary, life Maude had taken on to endure.

Pappy Ocain parked beside another truck, dull red with slat sidebodies, and before he could cut the engine, Cliffie opened the door and dumped Pee-Jean to the dirt. She landed like a cat on both bare feet, running.

Cliffie's dress, freshly pressed that morning, was hopelessly wrinkled. She smoothed the skirt as she slid out. Frowning, as she crossed the yard to the church front, she thought how all of the irksome things they did and said—even Pappy Ocain's sullen silence—served to alleviate her guilt. She couldn't wait to go and with good reason. But right now she dreaded walking up the church steps and through the double-doored shafts of sunlight, head hung to keep from facing Brother Leroy.

Inside, the chapel-sized church smelled musty, even with the wind rushing through the walls of open windows. Rows of shellacked pine pews, yellow in the sun, flanked the center aisle. There was talk of carpeting the hardwood floors after the church finished paying off the fake-oak paneling. Cliffie had been relieved when someone suggested wiring the old kerosene lanterns to electric instead of putting in fluorescent lights. Though she detested the lack of modern contrivances in the old house where she lived, she hated the thought of making new-like the old church house.

Listening to shuffling feet behind, Cliffie stared ahead at the pulpit, and like a sign popping up to remind her of what was bearing down on her mind, Brother Leroy stood from behind the podium and placed a sheet of paper on the slanted top.

She couldn't take her eyes off him, couldn't help it; he nodded and sat in one of the altar chairs, reading from the adult Sunday-school book. His face was blank—she didn't know what she'd expected, but it must have been precisely this: delay. Time for her to set things right with Roy Harris. Time for Brother Leroy to make it through one more Sabbath, Sabbath *day*, coming to a halt tonight. She felt like she was bleeding inside, could taste blood like orange Kool-aid.

Mrs. Ada Colridge's cane tapped up the aisle, behind Cliffie, while Maude, keeping pace, listened to the story of the old lady's gallbladder operation.

"I've still got a hurting in my left side," Mrs. Ada said.

"Yes 'um, I declare."

They moved up on Cliffie's heels—couldn't help but see her—and that Mrs. Ada didn't reach out and flip Cliffie's skirt tail with her cane was a sure indication that she'd heard the rumor and was shunning Cliffie.

Turning at her usual pew on the left, Cliffie slid all the way to the end, next to the window. In the blinding sun, she felt less conspicuous. Hands held stiffly on her lap, she sank into the heat. Maybe the sun worked to highlight her, like the bobby pin and the hair on her bedroom floor.

If she was lucky she might get to stay with Roy Harris two whole hours, first Sunday school, then church. It might take both hours to persuade him to take her to Fort Bragg. If asked later, she could always claim to have been sick in the outhouse. Somehow, she didn't think she'd be asked today.

"I got my eyes on you this time," Mary Helen said, popping into the sun and plopping down next to Cliffie.

Cliffie stared at her as she stared ahead, blond cheek hair accented by the sun.

"Mary . . . ," Cliffie started to plead, but paused. Mary Helen wouldn't be open to a plea, not from Cliffie, was nobody to confide in. Not that anybody would believe Mary Helen, especially not Pappy Ocain. She knew it too and was jealous of his taking Cliffie's word. Or maybe now that he no longer trusted Cliffie he'd sent Mary Helen to play keeper.

Cliffie got up and moved to the pew behind.

Mary Helen rose, smirked, and followed Cliffie, knocking knees as she wedged between pews. She sat, seeming to forget Cliffie as she leaned toward Jacko Prescott on the other end and started jabbering.

Cliffie stood and moved back another pew, then another, with Mary Helen following to the last pew in the shadowy corner.

While they were changing pews, the Sunday-school superintendent began reading the scripture for the day. Both Cliffie and Mary Helen sat at attention, Cliffie sighing and Mary Helen breathing in smug snorts. "You better look out, sister!" she warned and elbowed Cliffie.

"What's it to you?" Cliffie whispered, moving her arm.

"I tell you what," she said. "Roy Harris Weeks."

"Huh?" Cliffie grew weak.

"Me and Roy Harris," said Mary Helen. "We been going together, and I ain't letting him out of my sight till we leave."

"Oh, my God!" Cliffie swallowed hard, face to the wall. "No, Lord!"

"Yes, Lord!" Mary Helen seemed to be listening to Mr. Sam ask if anybody'd had a birthday the week before.

"Lord help us," said Cliffie in a toothachy tone.

"Right-O!" said Mary Helen.

"Give me one hour to break up with him."

"Nope," said Mary Helen. "You go out, I go with you."

"You do know I'm gonna have a baby?" Cliffie eyed the apelike contours of Mary Helen's face—inset brow, and from the nose down, protrudant.

"Yep," she said, still gazing off. "Everybody else do too."

"Do you know who the daddy is?"

"Shore do."

"Who?"

"Roy Harris Weeks."

"Don't that bother you—I mean that he's got me P.G.?"

"Yep, but it don't make that much difference," Mary Helen said. "I'm catching that bus with him in the morning."

"No, you're not, you little brat!" whispered Cliffie, hot-eyed.

"Watch me!" Mary Helen got up, as Mr. Sam dismissed everybody to the Sunday-school classes.

Cliffie stood and started around the pew, ahead of Mary Helen, brushing her hand along the wall as she went, and tried to look normal—in dread of Sunday school. Quickly, she shot along an empty pew, up the aisle, and out the front, not looking back, and hardly caring if Mary Helen, Pappy Ocain, or the whole church tailed her. She hopped off the stoop and darted across the yard. As she came around the corner of the Sunday-school wing, heading toward the woods at the rear, she spied Mary Helen at the door: face white, eyes wild, and mouth open with silent cursing.

"You!" Mary Helen hollered, just as Pappy Ocain's disfigured hand shot out and yanked her inside and slammed the door.

Stunned, Cliffie wondered if he'd seen her too, what he'd thought, but she didn't care as long as he didn't follow. Mary Helen would probably blab her head off, Cliffie thought at first, but decided her blabbing was unlikely under the circumstances.

Cliffie felt weak and light in the hot, growing sun, her

only consolation in knowing Mary Helen would want Pappy Ocain to believe that Brother Leroy was the daddy of Cliffie's baby, so he wouldn't kill Roy Harris. Mary Helen couldn't very well leave with a dead man. Good. Cliffie would have enough time now to do what she had to do, but she didn't now know what that was: surely murder if she heeded the hot blood burgeoning behind her eyes. She broke a switch from a gallberry bush while following the path through the woods.

Yes, she'd love to kill Roy Harris—her jaws locked, her neck was stiff as a joint of stovepipe. She felt like a fool. She'd always believed that Mary Helen was so readable, so see-through. Roy Harris, too. That he had divided his time equally between her and Mary Helen, setting them on the same scale, made Cliffie madder than anxious.

She walked faster, beating the soft black dirt with her feet, and imagined Mary Helen using the same path. Cliffie's path.

No wonder he was having such trouble deciding what to do; both she and Mary Helen had been pressuring him to take them. Had he even been trying to decide, or only trying to get away? At least Mary Helen wasn't pregnant—though it wouldn't surprise Cliffie. Her sister seemed superior now, and before there had been no contest—Mary Helen had been only one of Cliffie's pesky sisters, a minor hindrance. A minor hindrance!

Cliffie ducked under a maple tree, dainty notched leaves brushing her face. Mary Helen took a front seat in Cliffie's mind, along with Roy Harris. Her stomach didn't even stick out. Cliffie ground her teeth, grabbed her stomach. "Poor baby," she said, "I didn't mean it against you." Hearing words, volumeless in the closure of woods, and feeling the down pull of the baby, the muscles in the calves of her legs cramp, she felt drawn to sit on a stump and bawl, to stay there. But thinking of Mary Helen and Roy Harris, how she hated them both, spurred her on.

With her switch, now stripped of leaves, she scraped at yellow flies, swarming and biting her face, neck, and arms. She let them have her legs, which scissored through the myrtle bushes and palmettos where the path narrowed. Always before, she had shrunk away from the overgrown path and picked around for clearings till the path opened again. Now, she crashed through, still scared of snakes, but not as scared as mad.

The ground sloped to a grassy dale, where a black-water branch threaded through the woods. The air off the water felt cool and tart on her hot face. She felt sticky all over but didn't care that her bra molded to her breasts.

"Damned Roy Harris!" She'd cursed on Sunday. Was Aunt Teat at Sunday school? She couldn't remember, couldn't pull up Teat's face from the church crowd, with the blood pulsing hot, bright sparkles setting the leaves on fire. It didn't matter. If she had to, Cliffie would tell Teat off too. She wiped her face on the hem of her skirt, streaking it brown with powder.

Bounding toward the end of the path, which branched into Aunt Teat's dirt road, Cliffie heard a dove cry—hoped it was a dove and not a leak springing from her crying heart. She hoped she wouldn't cry when she got to Roy Harris's, hoped she'd stay mad, wished for a gun instead of a switch.

She'd given herself to him—so had Mary Helen. Cliffie felt the give of a little pity for her sister, which quickly went away. She couldn't bear to equate herself with Mary Helen, who wasn't even pregnant. Cliffie would have dumped Roy Harris in a minute if she wasn't pregnant herself. Now she was bound to him; Mary Helen was free. Maybe nothing serious had happened between them, nothing like . . . doing it. Cliffie doubted that. Roy Harris never went halfway.

She might as well admit it—she'd been used. She let go with a long breath, relieved after so long a time without admitting she'd been used. She'd suspected as much. She'd been only another girl to pass the time with; so had Mary Helen; so had crazy Emmacee. Who else?

As she tramped out of the bushes to the road, a branch

snagged her ponytail and snatched the ribbon loose, and she left it hanging—Mary Helen's ribbon, a hank of her own hair. He should die for what he'd done.

Keeping a steady gait, though her heels were blistering, she passed Tinion's house, ignoring the spotted hounds that yipped along the wire fence. She shook the switch as they pawed the wire and bayed. The low square house was still the way a house is with everybody gone, the yard neat but uneven with dog-dug holes. Frilly pink crepe myrtles grew on each side of the screened-in front. Cliffie knew Tinion was at church—he never missed a Sunday. She thought of the church with him there, with Pappy Ocain there, with Brother Leroy there, and Mary Helen surrounded by them all as she told where Cliffie had gone. She wouldn't. Cliffie relaxed again, tensed again, got so used to the pull and let-go, the two blended.

She'd always known Mary Helen was a fool. What did that make Cliffie? Double fool. Emmacee Mae was crazy, which gave her a good excuse for getting mixed up with Roy Harris Weeks. But with a good head on her shoulders, as Pappy Ocain put it, Cliffie should have known better. He'd tried to tell her.

"Oh, God!" she said. "Me and Mary Helen. What will Pappy Ocain say now?" Her troubles doubled.

"Roy Harris Weeks!" she hollered, spying the silvery boards of the shotgun house through the pine saplings in the side yard.

"Roy Harris!" she called louder, throat tightening with the pent-up name. She cleared her throat and walked tall, switch in hand. "You better get out here in a hurry, you sorry . . . !"

She thought the curse word, but wouldn't say it, feared going too far. She'd seen him in the blink of an eye snap from a light to a dark mood. Week before last, she had made the mistake of telling him that Pappy Ocain had told Tinion that Roy Harris had probably been responsible for setting fire to Tinion's cow barn. As soon as she'd said it, she wished she hadn't. Roy Harris exploded, lashing at the air with his arms. "Me? Me? I'm the one helped put it out," he yelled. "Hadn't been for me Tinion's mulafucking house would've burnt down." He snorted, reared, and stomped. "They looking for trouble out of Roy Harris Weeks, that's the way to start it." And she could almost picture him sticking a match to the hay, then slinking away from the barn, and dashing back when everybody in the flatwoods had gathered to help outen the blaze. She erased the picture from her head, like chalk on a board, till only white streaks showed.

Between the gap of two tall pines, she saw Roy Harris idle out to the front porch: black hair gleaming like tar, naked to the waist, khaki pants riding low, snatched on and left unbuttoned at the top, showing a patch of dark hair at his sucked-in navel.

Looking up at the sunny road, at Cliffie storming toward him, he didn't look so bothered as tough, ready for anything. He shook his head, glanced back at the door, and ambled off the porch, plopping to the doorstep.

"Roy Harris Weeks!" she shouted, coming quick, with the switch swinging. "How dare you?"

"How dare me what?" Elbows propped on his knees—the khaki shade of his pants washing over him—his hands hung loose between.

She knew he was mad from the cut of his eyes, brown as whiskey-bottle glass. "You," she started, switching the air before his face.

He snatched the switch, snapped it, and whacked her wrist smartly with the thick end. "Now shut up."

She did.

Gazing at her wrist, beginning to wheal, she waited for the red streak to fire her again.

"Set your ass down," he said, nodding to the doorstep.

"No, I—"

"Set down," he said, not even looking up, just saying it as if he wouldn't bother saying it again.

She sat, hearing the slither of the children on the floor inside, nearing, at the door now. The streak on her wrist swelled; the sting turned to throbbing.

"Get on back in yonder!" Roy Harris scolded and swatted the floor and three wet, twisted fingers with the switch. A dual-purpose grunt of pain and pleasure was loosed on the air.

Cliffie fixed her eyes on the rusty wire fence across the road. The fence sagged between posts with boughs of yellow honeysuckle, its sweet smell clashing with sulfur, rancid lard, and pee from the house. The porch was roofless, shaded only by a canopy of houseflies. A gully of sour dishwater mud, drying scummy white, ran from the back to the front yard.

Though she despised Roy Harris, she could feel pity growing on the periphery and reach her core. The throb in her wrist was almost gone, along with the pee smell and grunting behind. The screen door was sprung wide, stuck on a warped board. She wanted to get up and close it, to keep the children in, so she wouldn't have to see them and they wouldn't make Roy Harris madder than he already was.

Roy Harris started to say something, then jerked around, jumped up, and stamped inside. Cliffie heard the raw smack of flesh on flesh, followed quickly by a fierce grunt and Roy Harris cursing. On the porch again, he said, "Goddamned bunch of slobbering cripples," and sat. "I oughta knock 'em in the head and be done with it."

"No," Cliffie said, "don't . . . don't even say that." She knew he wanted her to beg him—his oily face beamed with sly pride—one of their games. Her duty as his better was to save him from himself.

"Now, if you got something to say to me, you better spit it out," said Roy Harris, "but keep a civil tongue in your head, you hear?"

"What about you and Mary Helen?" she said.

"What about us?"

Cliffie dared a glance at his snide, dark profile. His bearded jaw twitched. "Have you been going with her?" she asked.

"Hell, no!" He tossed his head, laughed. "Who the hell told you that?"

"She did," Cliffie said, spirits lifting, not yet won over, but trying and finding, in spite of his dangling denial, she didn't believe him, had so few choices. "She said it a while ago."

"Well, she's a bald-faced liar!" He cut the laugh, held Cliffie with his eyes. "That's what your little sister is, a bald-faced liar. I'll say it to her face."

"She said she's going with you to Fort Bragg tomorrow. Said she was catching the bus at Walters's store with you," Cliffie said, still not believing but going along because she had so little—nothing at all—to gain by not doing so. Besides, she knew she'd believe him before she left. Knowing that seemed important, also it was important that she hold tight to her unbelief, because truth, though sometimes impossible to tell from a lie, lurks somewhere. To part with that, she would be doomed. But wasn't she doomed anyway?

"That girl's crazy as a bedbug!" he hooted. "I ain't never give her no call to think nothing like that." He darted the switch to the road. "I be a son-of-a-bitch if they ain't always somebody out to stick it to you."

He stomped down the doorsteps and scuffed the dirt with his yellowed toes. Hands rammed in his pockets, he gazed off at the woods, as though amazed by the general inequity of things in general. He sighed, long and whipped, and ruffled his hair. "I reckon I might as well go on and tell you, seeing as how that dern gal's done ruint everything anyhow."

"What?" Cliffie said, playing, knowing she was playing, he was playing, waiting for the next line.

"I was gone surprise you by asking you to go with me to Fort Bragg. Course we'd get married." He turned, hesitating, eyes concentrated on her face as he dug in his pocket. He pulled out a thin gold band, crusted half-way around with pinpoint diamonds. "I want you to have this for a engagement ring."

Cliffie recognized it as Aunt Teat's; he recognized her recognition. "Teat give it to me to give to you, said she didn't have nare use for it no more." He matched faces with Cliffie, stiff bottom lips curling at the corners. Their eyes never batted.

"You mean it, don't you?" She crept down the steps toward him.

"That's up to you," he said. "I don't reckon you'd want to marry no man you couldn't trust. Would you?"

"I trust you—I trust you to tell me the truth." She lied about the truth, bargaining with herself: a lie for a truth, a truth for a lie.

"Thank you. I'm very happy," she lied, but she did thank him, knew she'd get on that bus, had to, would have to coddle time till the next morning. Time was as delicate as the hands on a watch; one slip of a cog and she could be left telling time by a stopped watch.

"What time do we leave?" She kissed his salty face.

He pulled her close; her neck jerked.

"Six or seven in the morning," he said.

"Which?"

"I don't know."

She would be there at five on the dot.

4

Waiting for night church to start, Cliffie sat in her usual pew and fanned with a cardboard hand fan, compliments of Roper's Funeral Home, Jasper, Florida—"You have our deepest sympathy." Each flutter of air passing over her like warm water. In science class, she'd learned that exerting energy makes you hotter. She fanned anyway.

She wished she could get up and leave, but she was too tired, too afraid. Her jaw felt locked, she itched all over, and the baby was a steady rolling reminder of why she had to stay put and see to the end this endless day. It seemed like a week. She had to keep reminding herself that things were progressing, that time, with the progress of the lazy sun, kept moving.

Preaching would start soon. The sun would set. Cliffie would watch through the two windows over the pulpit to see it sink behind the tilted tombstones in the cemetery. Then night. Then morning. Then the bus bound for Fort Bragg. The plan seemed so simple stacked like that, but time got in the way, time measured by minutes ticking off in her head, along with everybody waiting to thwart the plan.

Mary Helen came in and sat behind her.

Cliffie could feel eyes on the back of her neck. She turned just enough to see Mary Helen's face, red and puffy, shiny from crying.

All afternoon, she'd been boo-hooing and coughing in the

bedroom, skipping dinner and supper, while Cliffie sat at the table with the rest of the family, straining to act normal in the abnormal quiet. Maude and Pappy Ocain had eaten both meals bowed over their plates while the children nibbled and worried over Mary Helen's choke-and-cry act. Her pain had given Cliffie great pleasure.

Gave her pleasure now. Because she took Mary Helen's crying to mean she'd given up. Cliffie knew she'd be rubbing it in, but she would like nothing better than to slip Roy Harris's ring on her finger and scratch the back of her head for Mary Helen to see. But Cliffie couldn't afford to rub it in yet—the wind, static now, could still change. Besides, Roy Harris had warned her not to wear his ring because somebody might catch on that he, and not Brother Leroy, was the daddy of her baby.

So far, Brother Leroy hadn't denied anything. What a fool, Cliffie thought, glad fools were abundant, which made things so much simpler for smart people like her and Roy Harris. She smiled, knowing that the thought like the smile was fake: she ached all over just thinking about what she'd done to Brother Leroy and his family, how disappointed Pappy Ocain would be when he found out the truth.

Mary Helen sniffled and scraped a songbook from the rack at Cliffie's back. Her crying had graduated to mewing, exhausting in puffs through her nose.

Separating herself from the racket behind, Cliffie thought about Roy Harris's prompting that morning in Aunt Teat's yard. If she knew what was good for her, she'd make the lie stick. He had to hand it to her, he'd said, he couldn't have come up with an idea that good that quick. Yeah, it bothered him too, having to let the preacher take the rap, but it was that or get killed. Ocain Flowers wouldn't no more kill a preacher than he would his own mama!

Ten till seven, now. Church would start at seven. Already, everybody was straggling in, distraught, quiet, eying Cliffie.

Let 'em eyeball you; they can't eat you, Roy Harris had said when she'd tried to get him to hide out with her in the woods till Monday. Anything to keep from going to church that night and doing just what she was doing right now, shaking inside with fear and shame. She fanned harder and set her eyes above the pulpit. The sun still hung ripe in the tree-tops.

She cleared her throat.

Mary Helen coughed, sniffled.

Miss Dassie sidled between pews, ahead of Cliffie, and sat with a rocking motion. She turned to get a fan from the rack behind and, catching Cliffie's eyes, nodded, then faced the front again.

Mr. Sam shuffled in behind Miss Dassie, hiked his pants legs, and sat. Usually, he'd turn around and pick at Cliffie and Mary Helen, calling Mary Helen "cabbage head" and Cliffie "wormy." Now, he sat, turning his straw hat in his hands.

Cliffie could almost hear his thinking: he would have no part in the judging and sentencing of one of God's men. That would be his stand. He was a deacon, followed the law of the Bible to the letter, or as best he could—he didn't claim to be perfect.

Cliffie felt empty, dread building in her chest, ears tuned to the racket of children outside. Also filtering through the window were grown-up voices—same before-church talk as after church—and she fought back the urge to look out. It always amazed her how fast rumors spread among the spread-out flatwoodsers, as if on airwaves, and now they were gossiping about her. Her face glowed and gave off heat like the sun, promising to set. She sat straight, telling herself that everybody, including Pappy Ocain and Maude, was out politicking against the preacher, who was the guilty one, and not Cliffie, who was innocent, trapped and used.

She thought about the last preacher, a few years ago, who'd left before being asked (being *asked* to go was the same

as being told to go). She couldn't think of his name, only that
he'd been an edgy, slight man, who'd had a hard time keeping to the point of his sermon. One morning he just blew up
because K.C. had bounded out the door during the sermon to
kill a black snake crawling across the church yard. In defense
of all boys, Mr. Sam had declared that no normal boy in South
Georgia would have done different. But, he said to the boys,
from now on y'all see if y'all can't set still till the preacher
gets done. They never could—girls either. Out and in, to the
spigot at the pumphouse. Then the pump would clank and
hum for five minutes, between uses, refilling the tank, while
the preacher preached above it.

So far, Brother Leroy had managed to ignore the pump, as
well as the double doors—screen doors only, in summer—
which screaked open and slammed to while he sweated out
the gospel through his pores.

If ery one of mine was to be up-and-down, in-and-out,
while the preacher was preaching, I'd wear the flinder-rackets
out of them, said Pappy Ocain, who always sat in the second
pew from the front with Maude and the babies, and whose
children, especially Pee-Jean and K.C., kept the doors clapping
and the pump clanking and humming.

Five till seven. Pee-Jean pranced in and sat next to Cliffie and
crossed her arms on top of the pew ahead.

K.C. loped in behind her and perched at the end, waiting
for Pappy Ocain to come in so he could go out again.

Miss Oveeta, the pianist, waddled up the aisle to the black
piano with splintering veneer and settled in on the bench. She
propped a songbook open between two others and sank her
fingers into the yellowed ivories. The first notes of music,
coming on waves of mumbling, startled Cliffie. For all of her
having observed Miss Oveeta—having witnessed her warm-up
a thousand and one Sundays and knowing her next move like
the trill of the piano—she felt the shock of notes swell inside

her and threaten to flush onto her seat. She needed to go to the outhouse. She squeezed her thighs and shuddered, telling herself she didn't really need to go—already the center of attention, her getting up would call more attention—but her bladder was pressing against the baby, a fluid churning of its own. At the same time, she was trying to keep from looking out the window to see if the two voices she feared most coming together were whose she thought. If she didn't look out, like Lot's wife looking back on Sodom and Gomorrah, maybe God would spare her. But not looking was like already being turned into a pillar of salt.

There they were. Pappy Ocain and Brother Leroy, standing close under the black gum by the pumphouse. One nodding while the other talked, and vice versa. Both solemn faces fired by the saffron sun.

Oh, my Lord, Cliffie thought, they're making up, maybe talking about me and Roy Harris. Pappy Ocain *does not* believe Brother Leroy is the daddy. She had to get to Roy Harris before Pappy Ocain, but she couldn't go out the front or the back—not yet.

She stared ahead, hoping her ear to the window might pick up what was said. And though she couldn't hear for the tinkling piano and feet scratching sand into the church floor, she knew they were talking as they'd talked yesterday in the woods, maybe running the problem back through in search of a solution. Solution! What solution? Brother Leroy couldn't *marry* Cliffie. And Cliffie didn't really believe Pappy Ocain would go along with the idea of sending her to Witch Seymour.

When she could no longer hear the run-on murmur of voices, she looked and saw Pappy Ocain walking toward the front of the church and Brother Leroy shambling toward the Sunday-school wing. That Pappy Ocain had gone around the front meant he'd either decided not to bother Roy Harris, would let the preacher take the blame, or that he was going to the truck for his shotgun, possibly hidden behind the truck seat.

In a few minutes, Pappy Ocain and Maude passed along the center aisle, straight-faced, straight ahead, Pappy Ocain going before Maude, who paced a tow-haired toddler while cradling the baby in her arms. As Pappy Ocain started to sit, second pew from the front across the aisle, he looked back at Cliffie, eyes ancient and unforgiving, and wagged his head.

Cliffie felt faint, face draining white, and all that kept her from going out was the sound of Mary Helen sobbing behind. If Cliffie turned around now, they'd probably get in a fight. If she didn't, Mary Helen might work herself up into a confession. Cliffie would sit still and take her chances. One more good reason for not wearing the ring: let Mary Helen believe she stood as good a chance of getting on that bus as Cliffie. Mary Helen could go either way once the singing started— gospel music always brought out her pious side. But any music would do to get Mary Helen going. She loved to dance.

When they used to go to Twin Lakes with the Cornerville Baptist Church on Sunday-school picnics, Mary Helen would shag out on the pavilion dance floor, flared skirt furling about her thick calves. Swinging her curly head and dimpling her chin, she'd beg somebody, anybody, to come dance. All the boys would wander off, smirking, and Dottie Jean Belt, her best buddy, would finally mince out timidly in her black ballerina shoes to dance with Mary Helen.

Twenty miles from home and their only chance to swim, Twin Lakes had seemed as far away, as huge as the ocean. Now, if Cliffie and her sisters saw a body of water, it was a puddle following a sloshing rain, or black water backed up in a slough, Tom's Creek, on the way to church, or the creek-width Alapaha River, west of Cornerville.

Last summer, they'd got the scolding of their lives when Pappy Ocain had caught them in the river, where they'd sneaked off without him to squat on the bank and guard.

Splashing in the amber shallows, they'd seen him lope down-bank, along the coarse white sand, and stop to crop a willow switch—face red, a swiftness in his feet they'd never seen. All of them squealing, him shouting, they'd scampered ahead and up the bank, switch smarting their legs beneath wet, clinging skirts.

"Y'all come in a wan of getting drownd," he'd preached, parading them right through Cornerville to the house.

Out of the corner of her eye, Cliffie watched Emmacee Mae come in and scoot toward Mary Helen, scanning the church with her pinkish-green eyes. Midway of the pew, she began whispering, "Mary Helen, hey! Mary Helen Flowers, look here a minute. You got ery notion how come Brother Leroy's fixing to get run off?"

"I can't talk just yet." Mary Helen sniffled.

"What's ailing you?" Emmacee asked. "You sick or something?"

Mary Helen whimpered.

"Cliffie Mae?" Emmacee tapped Cliffie on the shoulder.

Cliffie could smell her sick-sweet sweat mingled with cheap, flowery talcum.

"Your sister back here's bawling to beat all. What's the matter with her?"

Cliffie turned around.

Mary Helen's face was buried in her hands, tight curls shaking. Emmacee's long arm hooked about her shoulders.

Cliffie shook her head and placed a finger on her mouth, nodding toward the front.

A soft squeak and clap sounded from the front door and Aunt Teat crept in and took her place in the right rear pew, next to the aisle. She always tended the door during preaching, and from time to time, Brother Leroy would make reference to her contribution from the pulpit, emphasizing how important it was for someone to tend that door. Tinion would get to church an hour early each Sunday morning and night—even on Wednesdays, before prayer meeting—to ring the bell, reminding everybody to drop what they were doing. But tending that door was just as important, Brother Leroy would say (Cliffie often wondered if he was hinting about everybody's slack, as he always hinted to prevent offending, so easily were most of them offended). They all served God's purpose, he'd say: most born-again believers, some only churchgoers—members of the church, playing church. Only God knows the heart. It's the inside of man that matters, like David, small David, son of Jesse. God looks on the heart of man, Brother Leroy would say, and hypocrisy will not be rewarded.

Seven o'clock, according to the square clock on the wall above the piano.

Lossie Adams, a short man with hair growing low on his forehead, stood behind the song leader's podium, small foot propped on the base. "Let's all get your red songbooks and open 'em to page 296—'Since Jesus Came Into My Heart.'"

Cliffie could hear Mary Helen singing, she and Emmacee trying to outsing one another. Mouthing words to the song, unable to avoid the duet at her back, Cliffie considered Mary Helen caterwauling in her ear. Usually, Cliffie would turn and shrink her with a sneer. But not tonight. Tonight, Cliffie shrank into herself, allowing petty annoyances free rein—until tomorrow morning at five o'clock. It was five after seven now.

During the opening prayer, Mary Helen started crying again.

"What's the matter?" Emmacee hissed.

Mary Helen coughed, sniffled; her curls trembled. Despite a full afternoon of crying, she'd found time to wet her hair and wind strands on paper-sack strips, then hung out the bedroom window for her curls to dry.

Pee-Jean looked around. "What's the matter?"

Mary Helen turned up the sniffling.

Cliffie sucked in. If one more person should ask, Mary Helen might burst out with everything, and it would all be over. "Shhhh!" she said to Pee-Jean.

The next hymn dried Mary Helen up again. Her favorite: "Bringing in the Sheaves."

Seven-fifteen. Cliffie's chest stung with fear, near-triumph. She decided to count the hours and hope while they sang "Living for Jesus."

Mary Helen cried harder, not even singing.

Pappy Ocain turned and eyed her, reddish brows drawing together. Cliffie started to look back too but knew one more look would rupture the dike. She chose to hope and count, culminating at five, Monday morning, with ten hours and fifteen minutes to go. Hold on, Mary Helen!

Brother Leroy stood in the pulpit to make announcements in his usual bland, apologetic tone. His voice cracked as he reminded everyone of the special-called business meeting after the service.

So, Cliffie thought, the church would be going on with the meeting, would ask him to leave. She hadn't seen Brother Leroy come in, but had known he was there, hidden behind the preacher's podium in one of the two altar chairs. Right under the picture of Jesus, who humbly surveyed all the hub-bub. Brother Leroy and Jesus.

Maude's baby bawled out of a building whimper, and she got up and tipped along the side aisle, brushing the wall with her fall-plaid frock.

Aunt Teat stood and opened one of the doors, chin on chest, eyes rolled up. Her face neither young nor old, not even in between. Before-age, an egg about to hatch.

Fifteen more minutes spent, give or take a few seconds, as the second hand swept round the square clock. Cliffie watched the hands sweep, relaxing every time Mary Helen's sobbing let up. Someone at the back had passed her a handkerchief, and she blew her nose in a satisfying gush. Did everybody think

Mary Helen was upset about the bad that had happened to her sister, or maybe what had happened to her *bad* sister?

Cliffie watched Brother Leroy, now seated in the altar chair. One brown loafer toe twitched to the music while he held his Bible on his lap. His lips parted, his eyes closed, and Cliffie knew he was praying. She searched the front pews for Sister Mary and the boys. She was glad they weren't there. Soon it would all be over; soon they'd be gone. Good! Let some old preached-out preacher, like the last, put up with this mess for a while. The next preacher would leave soon enough and another would come—there'd never been a preacher shortage before. It was a mystery to Cliffie how they searched out or stumbled upon this church, wooded in between Jacksonville, Florida, and Valdosta, Georgia—stateline hicks. Needmore, Fruitland, Pineland, Withers, and Tarver, shutdown sawmill and turpentine camps, settlements for the poor and rooted, the ignorant and the innocent, who found barely making it a privilege, a sacrament to the Lord.

Brother Leroy stood and cautiously stepped to the podium, placing his warped Bible on top with a lingering right hand. He paused, then spoke in a whisper that caught note and grew. As usual, he called out the chapter and verse of the text for them to follow, musing through the shuffle of pages with listless, lowered eyes.

Cliffie took a Bible from the bookrack and began turning the tissue pages to the book of Numbers, chapter nineteen.

"... impossible to keep the laws of God without the grace of the Lamb," Brother Leroy said, then read from those very laws, laws passed down from God through Moses:

And the Lord spake unto Moses and unto Aaron, saying,

This is the ordinance of the law which the Lord hath commanded, saying, Speak unto the children of Israel, that they bring thee a red heifer without spot, wherein is no blemish, and upon which never came yoke:

And ye shall give her unto Eleazar the priest, that he may
  bring her forth without the camp, and one shall slay her
  before his face.

And Eleazar the priest shall take of her blood with his finger, and sprinkle of her blood directly before the taberna-
  cle of the congregation seven times:

And one shall burn the heifer in his sight, her skin, and her
  flesh, and her blood, with her dung, shall he burn:

And the priest shall take cedar wood, and hyssop, and scarlet, and cast it into the midst of the burning of the heifer.

After reading nearly the whole chapter with him, the litany
of her own reading voice still singing in her ears, Cliffie
plugged into the sermon. At first, she felt satisfied that he was
sticking to a safe subject, but then caught on to where he was
going, and her face blazed.

My God! He was preaching about lust of the flesh. Was he
on the verge of telling the truth? *Lust of the flesh.* Did he say lust
of the flesh or lust of the *heart?* Why didn't he speak up for
himself? She almost wished he would, heard Mary Helen gasp
as he plunged on into lasciviousness, covetousness, greed, lust.
And just what did what he was preaching on have to do with
the scripture he'd just read?

To tell the truth, Cliffie knew he'd never laid more than a
holy hand on any of the women in the church. To tell the
truth, he was too shy and Christlike to even show interest. She
thought about his feverish hand, soft as a woman's, steering
her up the single, rickety doorstep and into the parsonage,
seeing her safely inside. His clean hand shaking hers, shaking
everybody's alike, as he stood by the door at the close of
every service. He even lowered his eyes if a woman smiled his
way, reserving that halting half-laugh for the men at dinners-
on-the-ground, closing spring and fall revivals.

Cliffie had often wondered about him and Sister Mary in

private. How had Sister Mary got P.G.? Twice! Cliffie had tried not to think about them that way, but she'd also wondered about Pappy Ocain and Maude, Aunt Teat, schoolteachers, Sunday-school teachers . . . Jesus. She'd almost come to believe that, like Mary in the Bible, those women got with child: immaculate conception. Not like her and Roy Harris, rough and struggling, searching for hot feelings like a dime behind a car seat.

Brother Leroy was sweating now, great drops popping on his high, wan forehead and rolling to his eyes, which he mopped with a folded white handkerchief.

Lust of the flesh, lust of the heart. He was still drawing the parallel.

Forty-five minutes down—it would soon be over. Cliffie looked forward to the church and her family sleeping six or so of the long hours left. She'd like to sleep herself, to drowse in the breeze playing through the window, where a black-husked beetle batted against the screen: ping, ping.

The door creaked and Maude crept up the wall aisle, cradling the sleeping baby, threaded through the pew, and sat next to Pappy Ocain. Aunt Teat spat off the stoop, and the door creaked to. The beetle circled the lantern above the center aisle and glanced off the hot bulb. *Impossible for man to keep the laws without Jesus.* The words rang out on Cliffie's mind, a litany reiterated by Brother Leroy and the locusts teeming outside. Black bug beating out the syllables against the bulb.

"Let he who is without sin cast the first stone," Brother Leroy said.

My God! Cliffie thought, he might confess to something he hasn't even done, young and fresh as he is.

Then he wandered to the edge of the platform—the altar no longer used for praying—and timidly rested a hand on the podium. "I want to confess something." He eyed Cliffie.

She gasped, sat forward.

"I'm guilty of lust of the heart, much as the next man

here. I reckon that comes with being human, and I'm a low-down, rotten sinner. I sin just breathing, and I deserve the cat-o'-nine-tails, the cross. I should leave; it's time. But I'd like to know if they's a man here amongst us ain't never lusted in his heart. Have we forgot the difference? Do we know there ain't no difference in lust of the heart and lust of the flesh?"

He let go of the podium and lifted both hands, underarm flesh showing red brier scratches from the chase through the woods. He raised his face, stretching taller, and brought both feet together. "While Miss Oveeta plays the invitation hymn, I want those of you that never committed lust in your heart to stay put where you are. Everybody else come up here to the altar and pray with me for forgiveness and for forgiveness for the next time, for the strength to at least try, to grow old enough, tough enough, inhuman enough to overcome."

Miss Oveeta began playing as Emmacee and a few other scattered voices led off on "Are You Washed in the Blood of the Lamb?"

After the first stanza, Cliffie expected Brother Leroy to close the invitation, remembering him always saying he didn't aim to beat nobody over the head with an extended invitation, but he went on into the second stanza, hands still raised, then a third, face lifted to the ceiling. She felt like going up there with him and shouting the truth, if for no other reason than for relief, but she reminded herself of what was at stake.

Orville Sapp rose, stumbled forward, tears rolling down his cheeks, and dropped to his knees at Brother Leroy's feet.

Directly, Slash Maine joined Mr. Orville, kneeling with one blunt knee cocked uncertainly for his elbow to prop on.

Two more stanzas and only Emmacee was singing; Cliffie thought surely Brother Leroy would let up. Eight-fifteen. He knew how they hated to be held over. And what about the special-called meeting?

Aunt Teat waddled toward the altar. She dropped to her

knees, the soles of her shoes spotted with gum, traces of mud. Her head bowed, young hair splayed on her rutted nape.

Miss Ella Faye came up and knelt beside her and placed a big rugged arm about her shoulders.

Then Pappy Ocain stood, hesitated, and shuffled forward, hiking his pants. He looked long at Brother Leroy, then started to take his place between Slash and Orville. But he turned back, mumbling, and shook Brother Leroy's hand. Brother Leroy tugged him nearer and hugged him, and at first Pappy Ocain stood stiffly, taking the embrace like a dose of medicine, then hugged Brother Leroy back.

Maude ambled to the altar, gathering the sleeping baby in her arms, another dragging on her skirttail, while Emmacee alone sang shrilly: "Are you washed in the blood, in the soul-cleansing blood of the lamb, are your garments spotless?"

Hair tightening at the scalp, Cliffie suddenly realized that something was missing and jerked around to face Emmacee and the empty pew where Mary Helen had sat. Emmacee started to cry, clapped her songbook on the pew, and lumbered toward the altar, toward the million-tongued prayers going up in a hiss to cancel out hissing for all time.

Cliffie didn't need to stop Emmacee, straggling past her, to ask where Mary Helen had gone. She knew. She waited for Emmacee to reach Brother Leroy, for his holy eyes to cast down as she knelt at the altar, then Cliffie dashed toward the double-screened doors, flung them open, and hit the dirt off the stoop. In the khaki dusk, prayers meshed with the crickets and lingered, dissolved. Her own mumbling loud in her ears, "I'll kill that devil," she said.

At the pumphouse, K.C. and a bunch of other boys were spewing each other with mouthfuls of water, but stopped to watch her cross the rake-marked yard toward the rear of the church.

She gazed out over the white tombstones, dusted with twilight, then ducked under a branch on the path through the woods, where the strains of crickets and katydids grew stronger, filled her head, made her ears ring. She felt confused by the light, a soft dappled gray beneath the black gums and bays. Was it dawn or dusk? In the dead air under the trees prickles of sweat made her skin feel like it was shedding.

"And I'll kill that little . . ." she said, leaving off the word *liar*, which Roy Harris had called Mary Helen just that morning, hardly believing he'd meant it anyway, though unable to afford not believing him. "The minute I turn my back . . ."

Still walking, she checked the path for tracks, found her own, coming and going, with another set woven through. The tracks were like a puzzle, and walking while looking down made her dizzy. Her back ached, her head filled with blood. She went on, running till her heel strings pulled.

She would put Mary Helen in her place, once and for all. How dare she! How dare she cry and mope around the bedroom all afternoon, locking Cliffie out? When Pappy Ocain and Maude had tried to sit on the porch after dinner, her bawling, carrying through the window and along the hall, had driven them back into the kitchen. How dare she sit in church like a saint and then sneak out!

Dusk quickly weakening and dark coming strong from the stands of pines, time now seemed to rush. Cliffie wondered what time it was, and what if she needed more time, rather than less, with this new kink in her plans?

"Mary Helen and Roy Harris." The names as a pair loomed like the dark over the dusk. Her voice rang foolish in her ears because, despite Roy Harris's denial, she knew he'd been seeing Mary Helen . . . more than *seeing*. She knew his denials, had often felt the nettle of his tricks.

As she neared the corner post of Mr. Tinion's fenced yard, she heard his dogs strike into excited barking. Confused faces quickening from listening stupors, ears perked, they looped and darted along the fence, then skidded in the torn earth at the corner where the cow pasture started.

Yellow-green grass covered the level field, like morning sun, up to the tree line that curved into woods, a deepening green, where dark would come stalking like a panther. Midway of the field, a line of cows grazed languorously toward the west fence. A butt-headed heifer, off to herself, stood belly deep in a black pond, lowing in measured bellows from a wreath of lily pads. Her eyes, mirroring the black surface, fixed on Cliffie, who'd stopped to dump sand from her shoes.

What would she do when she got to Aunt Teat's? Would she gain anything by bursting in on Roy Harris and Mary Helen? Maybe she should turn around now and just show up at the bus stop in the morning? Show him how much she trusted him. But she walked on, rehearsing how she'd act—sure, trusting, casual, just dropping by. Mary Helen would never buy such an act, but Roy Harris would go along with anything that didn't threaten him.

Nearing the shanty, she heard Mary Helen hoot, the sound falling sharp on the woods, like children playing after supper. Cliffie took a deep breath of tart air, swinging her arms as she walked, face stinging under the skin, cool on the surface from a lift of air. Over the patch of saplings, she could see Mary Helen and Roy Harris sitting together on the doorsteps, Mary Helen rocking her knees, arms crossed on top. Roy Harris, with his head hung, appeared molded of clay, chest naked, feet on the doorstep.

Cliffie thought of hiding behind the blind of fox grapevines that trailed from the crumbling log crib—she could learn more that way—but she was afraid of what she'd hear, couldn't risk it. She had to face them and yet close her eyes to what was going on. If she was as smart as Pappy Ocain said, she'd stay calm, no matter what. Closing in on the front yard, where the edge sloped to the road, she bit her bottom lip, reminding herself to be cool but aware of Mary Helen's goal.

Roy Harris's hands were dangling between his knees: same way he'd sat with Cliffie that morning. Same day. Mary Helen sat where Cliffie had sat, wearing the same look of desperation, hope. Cliffie could almost feel herself sitting in her sister's place. At that core where mean thoughts trundle, regardless, Cliffie hoped she hadn't looked like Mary Helen—coarse-featured, pebbly white against the swirling gray void of dusk. But she was forced to admit that theirs was the same stance, same position, same unbearable tension. They finally had something in common.

Mary Helen's face lifted and her gypsy eyes stretched wide. Her crying jag had ended. Spying Cliffie, she clutched Roy Harris's arm—maybe she'd been clutching it before, Cliffie couldn't tell. Their arms and legs were a confusion of limbs, dusk the fusion.

Roy Harris kept his head low.

Mary Helen said, "Look what the cat's drug up," in a tone straining toward cleverness, and kept holding to Roy Harris's arm.

He let her.

"What're y'all up to?" Cliffie said.

Mary Helen snorted, smirked.

Roy Harris still didn't look up, but Cliffie could tell he was frowning by the way his black eyebrows arched.

Mary Helen tucked her dimpled chin. "What you doing messing around here this time of day, Cliffie Mae?"

"Just out walking," Cliffie said. "Got stiff setting in church, business meeting and all coming up." Trumped-up truths getting easier.

She watched Roy Harris's eyes cut her way as she paraded over to Mary Helen's end of the doorsteps. She'd felt forced to choose a side, so she'd chosen Mary Helen's, because when Mary Helen got up Cliffie would sit.

"Being as how you the one they fussing over," Mary Helen said, "hadn't you better be there for the business meeting?"

"Not necessarily," Cliffie said, watching Roy Harris—neither for nor against. She feared, with a surge of fire in her chest, that he'd gone over to the other side. She pulled the twine necklace from her bosom and showed the ring.

Mary Helen flinched.

"Now, hadn't you better see if you can't make it back across them woods?" said Cliffie.

Inside the house, the floor creaked and gave with the wallowing weight of the children. Something fell—klock! One appeared behind the door, long fingers picking at the screen.

"You the one better get your tail back yonder to church," said Mary Helen. She let go of Roy Harris's arm, stood, and straightened the belt on her red polka-dot dress skirt. "Ain't that what you say, Roy Harris?" Smirking, she cut her eyes from him to Cliffie. Suddenly concerned with her hands, hanging loose alongside, she crossed her arms.

Roy Harris's face lifted from his knees. "I 'magine both y'all better get on back before somebody starts smelling a rat."

Eyes locked on Cliffie's ring, Mary Helen asked Roy Harris, "Did you give her that ring?"

"I give a bunch of girls rings," he said, tired and bored and rising. Stretching, his slick chest expanded, tallow in the dusk. "Now y'all get on out from here." He yawned as he ambled across the porch and through the screen door.

Before so devoid of commotion, the house came alive with music from the radio, the primitive grunting of the children, Roy Harris scolding them. Suddenly, he popped behind the screen door, gray-meshed, put-out and glaring. "Y'all get gone now!" Then vanished like a Halloween spook.

Mary Helen looked like she was puffing up—rouged cheeks and chest inflating. Swaying, her full skirt swished, starched crinoline and all. Lazy about most things, she always starched her crinoline at night, standing over a steaming pot of gummy Argo starch, then hung it on the clothesline by the tail, to fan just above the dirt in a sheer white circle, like the moon by day.

At school one day, a Georgia Boy grasshopper had got caught in the net and stung Mary Helen on the leg, and she'd shed her crinoline in the hall, shrieking to the world that a black widow spider had bit her. Embarrassed when somebody found the giant red-and-yellow-striped grasshopper, crippled by her beating hands, she'd still sworn that a spider had bitten her. For two days, she'd traipsed the halls, warning about a black widow on the loose. Said she'd been up sick all night.

Cliffie slept with her. She knew her. Sleeping with somebody tells a lot, Cliffie decided.

Red lips now set in a pout, Mary Helen said, "Well, what you got to say for yourself?"

"I'm pregnant," Cliffie said, seeming to hear the full significance for the first time, not meaning to plead, not meaning not to plead, just saying what came first, in hopes that her sister would do the right thing.

Mary Helen snorted. "I noticed that."

Cliffie wished she'd not stooped to begging; she felt like Teat.

"Y'all better be gone in a minute," Roy Harris yelled above the yodeling on the radio. "I ain't telling y'all again."

"What you want me to do about it?" Mary Helen said to Cliffie, smugly gazing off at the woods—oblivious of the rumbling house behind—and held her place on the doorsteps.

"Let things alone so me and my baby can have a chance," Cliffie said, self-charity piercing her chest, and knew better. But she had nothing better to go on; obviously, Roy Harris Weeks never intended to take either, had been stringing them along till he could skip town without Pappy Ocain's finding out.

Thinking how she hated him, how she should go straight to church and tell everything, she missed Mary Helen's last remark, one of those smart sayings she saved like some people save cash.

"I wouldn't put it a-past you!" Mary Helen said next, eyebrows arched, snagged on their pointless word sparring, their common purpose—Roy Harris, grumbling inside like the radio, only something going on.

Cliffie knew that Mary Helen had just accused her of getting pregnant on purpose to trick Roy Harris into marrying her, but the fact that Mary Helen had plucked all her eyebrows and drawn two reddish-brown arches in place seemed to take over. Her words, like her eyebrows, false.

Cliffie decided to drop the talk and simply show up at the bus stop, hoping for the best. But she almost hated the idiot inside, hollering above the radio; how could she go with him? How much better off would she be than Maude if she went? And Pappy Ocain—at least Pappy Ocain loved her, would take care of her and the baby. She listened to the fan whirring and rattling, the children grinding and grunting, a confusion of staticky country music. "I'm going back to church and tell Pappy Ocain to quit blaming Brother Leroy," Cliffie shouted. In a one-two beat, the words had tumbled out, caught on the air. Feet hit the floor inside.

Mary Helen gasped, "You wouldn't dare!"

"I'm not doing it to spite nobody," Cliffie said evenly, crying now. "It's just time to tell the truth, let Brother Leroy off the hook."

Day had turned to twilight, objects and people in confusion, light shifting, a warp of images and sounds. Time had extended, and darkness, even as it came, brought clarity by comparison. The up-and-down boards along the front of the house separated, easy to count between blackened cracks, and traveled to the eaves of tin, patchy with rust and dull spatters of light. Senses quickened, Cliffie perked to the blur of crickets, sharp and apart from the mad keening of katydids, the trill of tree frogs, no longer just a throb of night.

Thomas, one of Aunt Teat's children, spirited into the doorway and gyrated, long white neck elastic, then crawled away with a smile on his pulled-down face. The one called

Noodle filled the space behind the screen, peering gaily out, and flowed away with a thin baby laugh.

To keep from marking her baby, Cliffie focused on the broken-backed chair beside the door: minus two spindles, two intact, a four-spindle chair. Across the porch floor, she spotted the nail sticking up from a loose board that always snagged Roy Harris's pants cuff as he moped inside.

She'd never been past the living room of the house, was too sickened by the slavered floors, the heavy reek of grease and pee that emanated from the rose-patterned curtain partitions. The children glided beneath the curtains, caressed by the dirty hems.

Standing there, as in a dream of being alone in the world, she looked right at the child writhing in the doorway—Scram, she thought he was called. Her eyes met his, blank-blue. His uncontrollable features grew excited; he grunted and rollicked away, naked legs dragging. Feeling the spring of tears to her eyes, Cliffie thought about her own crying now and her crying before—the difference in the reasons behind crying now and crying then—thinking also that she'd stood there in the foot-tamped dirt off the steps for what seemed like hours, but knew it had been only minutes—maybe seconds—while the same thuds and bumps inside filtered outside. Mary Helen wore the same shocked look. The hillbilly song was the same. Cliffie felt like she'd been forty years in the wilderness with the children of Israel. She no longer hated Mary Helen; she hurt for her. Gray eyes glaring, arms unfolding and falling to her sides, she looked sincere suddenly, and Cliffie hardly recognized her without the airs.

"You can't tell yet," Mary Helen said. "Not yet."

Cliffie strained to connect the remark to the point where they left off speaking, forty years before.

Mary Helen's face was wiped clean as the clear, starring sky. "You can't," she repeated. "Pappy Ocain'll kill him." In slow motion, Mary Helen lifted one hand out to her sister.

Cliffie could no longer feel the ground under her feet; she seemed to float on waves of crickets and katydids. A song somewhere.

In the ghost of Mary Helen's lifted arm, Roy Harris appeared, a smirking spirit, bumping the screen door back with a five-gallon can. "See this here can of kerosene?" he shouted. "I got a box of matches in my other hand and ain't got nothing better to do but strike 'em."

Arms flapping, Mary Helen jumped from the steps and hollered out.

Lifting the can by the bottom with one hand, the other on the handle, he swung it toward her, a gurgling arc of kerosene raining to her tracks, then soaking like magic into the dirt. "I'll git you!" he hollered, and without so much as a look of warning, swung the can again at Cliffie to the left of the steps. She darted away, then eased back, transfixed by the oily flowers of kerosene blooming in the sterile earth.

"Y'all think I won't burn them bastards up?" Roy Harris nodded at the three mute faces in the doorway. They peered out, faces angular and white, all six hands grappling at the porch floor. Their bodies tangled as they wedged into the doorway. Roy Harris laughed, thick and vile, and slung an iridescent stream of kerosene from the can to the writhing bodies. They lapped and folded back, with trailing white legs and grunts.

"No, don't, Roy Harris!" Cliffie begged. "Don't. I won't say nothing." She started up the doorsteps.

Holding to the handle, he slung the can again and a singing streak of kerosene dashed from the spout to her, dolloping her blue dress and ribboning on the floor. She backed away, hands out, the streak on her skirt spreading.

"I'm gone take care of y'all in a minute," he said; then shouted, "I'm fixing to leave a sign says Roy Harris was here."

Mary Helen screamed, a haunting, distant sound, though

she stood just off the battle space between Cliffie and Roy
Harris. Then she ran, hollering, a running holler.

Cliffie locked eyes with Roy Harris; he laughed, something
thick working up from his throat.

"Please don't," she begged, begging too her trembling to
quit. "I'll go away and not never mess with you no more."

"I ain't got no guarantees you'd go on and let me alone so
I can get on that bus." His neck was strutted, eyes seething in
the scattering dusk. He shook the box of matches like a baby
rattle.

Cliffie tensed against the quick, bright light in his control.
"No, please don't." She stepped away. "I won't never tell
nobody, I promise."

"Like hell you won't!" His dark eyes darted on the air like
bats. "Get back in there," he hollered at the doorway, dashing
a half-circle of kerosene from the heaped bodies to his own
feet. He jumped away from the wet loop growing on the
floor. Fumes, sharp and oily, spread on the air with Mary
Helen's howls.

Roy Harris, stomping about the porch, seemed skittish and
confused, his madness undirected, all around. Cliffie felt that
she was no longer the object, that he couldn't even see her.
She crept closer while he doused the porch, left to right,
dousing her in the process, and touched his hot, slick rib
cage; and he slammed her shoulder with the gurgling can,
then reached for her, steadying himself to keep from slipping
on the oily floor.

Holding her shoulder and backing, she skated down the
kerosene-drenched doorsteps and landed on her elbows and
knees, jumped up and ran to the edge of the yard, hiding
behind a scraggly mimosa. At first, she thought she might cry,
then realized she'd gone beyond that to a tension much like
freezing: eyes fixed, teeth set, ears roaring deaf. She looked at
the dark border of woods, searching for Mary Helen, whose
hollering seemed to revolve in the circular stands of palmettos.

"Mary Helen?" she whispered. "Mary Helen, come here. Please, shut up, please! Come here." If Cliffie could find her, stop her, maybe he'd calm down and stop slinging the kerosene, not strike . . .

Roving about the woods, around the house, Mary Helen's howling reeled out, then in. Roy Harris cursed—sometimes in string of words that jabbed the eerie quiet, quiet rent only by Mary Helen's howls and the on-again, off-again music on the radio. Dollops of kerosene splashed on the floors, walls, and windows, taking the place of the radio as the children fiddled with the volume.

"Teach you Ocain-looking bitches to mess with me," Roy Harris shouted from the porch.

The radio loaded the air again, the song faded, and the unaffected disc jockey spoke in put-on country. A steady chorus of mutters was coming from the house, from the front and side windows, as Cliffie crept toward the back. Everything had gone blessedly dark, almost black. She dreaded the blasts of light and heat.

Stumbling in holes, she searched for the back porch. The house was a black block. Her teeth chattered, but she didn't feel cold, didn't feel pain and should, because she must have hurt herself when she'd slipped down the steps. She touched a bruised welt from wrist to elbow, but felt no pain because all feeling was absorbed by Mary Helen's howling and Roy Harris's cursing, so vile that the sounds merged, emerged as the darkest of darkness.

Nearing the back porch and feeling for the edges, she whispered, "Thomas, Scram, y'all come here, babies. Come to me."

"Y'all ready to see a big fire? Huh?" Roy Harris's voice in the front carried throughout the house. "Y'all ready?" He laughed, hoarse and mad, his laugh claiming the dark and the radio, the crickets, and Mary Helen's howls.

Where the woods started from the shallow back yard,

penned hogs snorted and squealed, sending crawling waves of sour-mud air.

Cliffie knew Roy Harris could no longer hear her, was absorbed in his own madness, so she didn't bother to be quiet. She clapped her hands, heard the children grunt just behind the closed door. Hoisting herself up, nose nearly touching the floor, she scrambled to her feet and felt for the wall, praying she'd not see it. "Open up the door, babies," she said sweetly. "Please open the door. Scram, I'm here; y'all don't be scared. I come to get you."

"Y'all fixing to see the biggest fucking fire you ever seen in all your born days," Roy Harris shouted.

Running hands along the cool, smooth wall, Cliffie listened for Mary Helen. "Stay back, Mary Helen!" she shouted, fumbling and finally feeling the door, then the knob, which turned freely without opening it. She turned the knob again, frantically bumping with her hip. Between bumps, she could hear the children grunting and scratching at the door.

"Noodle, one of y'all, unlatch the door. Unlatch the door." She turned the knob again, full double rotations, and heard it rattle, the children scratching at the door and mewing like kittens. She slammed the door with her shoulder and hip.

"Y'all ready?" Roy Harris hollered.

Cliffie heard the pounding of his feet as he jumped from the porch to the dirt, heard the snap of matches on the box. Resting her head against the solid dark door, she heard the clear, panicky breathing of the children, hogs snorting at her back, Mary Helen howling from the front, and matches striking . . .

"God, help me!" she cried, a burst of light whooshing from front to rear of the house.

Roy Harris laughed wildly and whooped, "Tell Ocain this one's on me." Mary Helen howled louder. The woods glowed.

Turning from the door, Cliffie dashed toward the glowering orange square of an open window at the other end of the porch. Ripping the wire screen at the edges with her nails, she poked her head through and, across the brilliant square table, saw the three children huddled, gazing up, and scrabbling at the door, bodies tangling like spaghetti. The kitchen, bright orange and glistening with kerosene, looked drab and gloomy, even with the fire tattering the rose curtains and gnawing the walls, the floor, the fire-stained children.

As Cliffie stuck her leg through the window, flames arced across the floor, a clean line of fire cropping up between her and the children, and gathered in the window, heat like the margin of hell. She fell back to the porch floor, screaming, flames pouncing full on like a wild cat. She could smell her own hair singeing, her dress scorching, hear hogs snorting, children grunting, Mary Helen hollering.

Beating at her hair, then her skirt, more an odor of scorch than a feel of burning, she scrambled up and darted from the lazy burning spot on the end of the porch to the door. She lunged and rammed the door till she couldn't move, then clawed at the edges, listening for the children. She could hear their shallow cries, her own moaning, the stinging of her thighs, face, and arms, pain rearing its head like a snake.

Banging her forehead against the orange-seamed door, she felt the heat and shared heat, pleading, it seemed, to get into the fire. She crumpled to the floor, cheek resting on the door, taking in the smoky fragrance, like a good oak fire in winter. She got still, listening to the roar of the fire diminish with the children's crying and grow overhead.

Smoke filled her head, a thick, gray spiraling she could see and feel, even hear as her ears clogged with plugs of smoke, sandy eyes melting to ruby-red glass, heat rushing over her, outside-in, from head to toe. She imagined standing back from the porch and watching her crumpled body twinkle and glow. She could smell her own flesh and thought how strange to smell herself burn, the body she knew so well by smell but had never thought of burning, of dying. And burning seemed alive, the opposite of dead.

"Jesus will come soon to put us out," she said softly. As she sucked deeper into herself, away from the red-white heat, a bracket like fired iron slid beneath her arms and locked around her chest, tugging backward—the fire backing off, not her, from the line drawn between herself and the burning.

"No, no," she screamed inside, ears hot and clogged, blocking sounds. Her heels dragged along the dirt, leaving dual red trenches, as the waving flames fell away. She struggled against the hot arms on her chest—she could see red hands on her breasts now and hear wailing, hot wailing—and with each lurch sideways, her armpits rubbed raw, breasts shredding like rotted cloth.

The red hands unhinged and dropped her next to a sprawl of palmettos. On her back, she stared at the sky, churning low with smoke. Beyond crying, wrapped in pain, she turned her head and felt her thinking self rise to the smoke, her feeling self still level with the dirt, eyes scanning the yard to the road through blood-tinted lenses.

Strange people scurried, shouting, their faces shocked open and shadowy, and fed into the yard lit by the naked neon frame of the house.

Somebody was crying over Cliffie, covering her legs to chest with a heavy, hot blanket. It hurt but didn't matter because she was hurting without the cover.

A woman touched her cheek. "Honey, you'll be okay."

She flinched, then tried to make out the other people who were crying behind, tiers of crying. "Somebody, run go get help, Cliffie's bad burnt," one said.

Cliffie gazed up at the boiling smoke; she knew the voices belonged to Maude and Sister Mary, but couldn't tell one from the other. It didn't matter. She needed to think. Mary Helen was no longer hollering; Roy Harris was gone—maybe dead. The absence of hollering and cursing eased the tightness along Cliffie's jaw, the crackle of fire seemed clean and purging, yet a terrible sundering of earth and sky.

Feeling able to levitate and sink at will, Cliffie rolled her head to one side, level with the bumpy dirt, and watched a colony of people trail from the warped brick well to the burning frame of the house, dashing buckets of water on the unhampered flames that ate down from the pitch of rafters, then loop back to the well, undefeated, like ants building a hill.

Somebody older, unable to run, lugged two buckets of water from the well. With a pang of recognition, Cliffie lifted her head, and followed Mr. Sam with her eyes to the house, half his face in shadow, half scalded red. It seemed so important to have found someone familiar, and yet so scary when she considered the two women crying above, whom she would not—could not—look at.

"I didn't mean for this to happen, Mama," Cliffie said through her teeth. "I'm sorry, I'm sorry"—hard words to get started, harder to stop.

"I know, honey," Maude said, sidestepping crying women, shouldering them aside like a mama dog with puppies. "Shhh now."

"Pappy Ocain," Cliffie said, the name dropping short between I'm sorrys.

"She's calling for her daddy," somebody behind Maude hollered against the roar.

"Ocain!" somebody else yelled. "Where's Ocain?"

Across the yard a man called, "He run back to get the truck, he's coming."

"He's coming, honey, he's coming." Maude stroked Cliffie's raw forehead, the way she used to do the bangs, making them stick up.

Her touch hurt, but Cliffie kept still. "Don't let him run, Mama; don't let him help put out the fire . . . his bad heart."

"Ain't his heart's a-worrying me right now, honey," Maude said, just like at home when she talked to herself through the children.

Several women and men from church, recognizable to Cliffie by shape but not by shadow-gutted faces, crowded around the south side of the house, a wall intact but smoldering, sending off jets of smoke. Helplessly, they shouted, danced up and away from the fiery window, as though taking turns peeping in.

Between the fire and Cliffie a sow scuttled across the yard, trailed by a litter of squealing pigs, punchouts in the brightness. They looked like hogs running from the burning woods on a sunny day.

The rear door swung wide on the blazing wall and Aunt Teat struggled out, her back feathered with fire like an orange shawl, cradling what looked like a bright patchwork quilt. She dumped the child off the burning porch into waiting arms and turned, face to the flames. Her eyes were like flaring wicks of candles.

The arms bore the treasure to the edge of the woods and released it, to settle hot next to Cliffie. The crying all around rolled back and Cliffie knew why, knew who was making up the row of dead, and waited with her eyes sealed against the light, accepting that she'd die too, until she couldn't stand not looking, then knew she wouldn't die but would wish she could.

She forced herself to watch the house, eyes glued where Aunt Teat again appeared and dropped her burden off the edge of the porch, unhampered by pleas and shot-out hands. Plodding mechanically, a living torch, she passed through the flaming frame and grabbed the last child, dragging him to the edge of the porch, where only a long foundation beam blazed, and rid herself of what she loved.

Cliffie heard Pappy Ocain's stiff, scratchy voice, odd in the backed-off crowd, not frantic and loose like everybody else's, but shaky-scared or mad. He came to her and knelt. She stared at his wild face. "Pappy Ocain?" She didn't know why she questioned.

He studied her. "I mought as well set fire to your big toe, gal," he said. His face looked like it had when he'd chased the preacher through the woods, and she was glad and scared at the same time, glad because his mad look meant he wouldn't let her die and he wouldn't die either, scared because how he looked, what he said, sounded like he hated her.

Pappy Ocain stepped aside as a man brought up the last child and laid it next to the others. Cliffie searched the face of the man and recognized Brother Leroy.

"Cliffie!" he said in a strangled voice, as if he'd finally come round to taking the name of God in vain.

Voices rose and they both turned to the house to see a cross of flaming rafters crash onto Aunt Teat's back as she lumbered off the edge of the porch.

Clutching themselves and stepping away, everybody grew quiet and watched while the whole house collapsed and the fire soared unhindered into ashes.

5

Standing at the bars of her jail cell, two months later, Cliffie imagined having seen the bus pull up at Hoot Walters's store that Monday, did indeed have a peep-out view of the concrete slope where the bus pulled up and out each Monday, as regular as the tick of time, leaving a ravel of smoke to the river bridge.

In the picture, Roy Harris stands with a foot propped on the bench out front, while Mary Helen in a yellow hat and dress saunters through the store door. The Trailways, white with red writing, waits for them to board, then pulls away as they sit, faces blue behind the blue-tinted window.

But that was before Brother Leroy came by and told Cliffie the truth—everything. The truth means always telling everything; less is a lie. No half-truths. Truth, told, also means that somebody must be protected. Cliffie would never tell, would protect Pappy Ocain from the altogether-truth forever.

She didn't know how bad his bad heart really was, but she knew that letting the whole world in on his shame could make a good heart go bad. His pinched face seen daily through the bars served as a reminder that one more shock, one slip, could kill him. Having to talk through bars was hurt enough.

She'd stay with the half-truth and spare him, no matter what. And she'd have her baby, no matter what.

■ ■ ■

Her face was healing into slick, raised scars and pits, her lips into the shape they'd burned, curled like melted plastic; her eyelids no longer closed, never permitted complete peace of sleep. She didn't worry about the scarring—the doctor had said they'd do "cosmetic surgery." Alongside her other troubles, how she looked no longer mattered.

Let my baby be all right. The tight litany sang in her heart as she waited on the cot of the one-cell jail.

The law believed she'd set fire to Aunt Teat's house, as Roy Harris had claimed that night. He'd told she did it out of spite, believing that he was inside, because he wouldn't have anything to do with her. Let Leroy Crosby take care of that crazy, it's his youngun she's toting. Roy Harris Weeks hadn't never laid a hand on none of Ocain's girl younguns. They weren't his type. It wasn't his fault she was always chasing after him. Go ask Emmacee Mae.

Cliffie hadn't heard him say that. She'd been in Little Griffin Hospital, in Valdosta: ears storming, eyes blazing in their sockets—pain too great to lose or hold. Pappy Ocain part of that lapse in living, framed against a parchment plaster wall. She'd welcomed the sharp smell of ointment and the clean of white bandages, at last covering the stink of burned flesh. Sick and dazed, the taste of ether cold on her tongue, she had watched Pappy Ocain pray, head low but lifting now and then to say, "It'll be all right, sugar." Praying through the all-night, sitting spraddle-legged till he grew into the wall like a picture hung when she got there.

Brother Leroy had filled Cliffie in on the details. She could imagine Roy Harris telling his side and knew everybody took it for a half-truth, but her side—had she been able or known to tell it—was no more or less.

The evening of the fire, one of the boys out at the church pumphouse had overheard Cliffie threaten to "kill that devil." One of the women had heard her say, "I didn't mean for this to happen"—she had said both, just words. And according to at least half the church, she'd lied on a man of God. They had divided over whether she'd actually *been with* the preacher, or lied, or led him on, rumor taking hold till truth made no difference. Her word was no good.

And Brother Leroy, who knew the truth, would never tell. Neither would Cliffie. She'd die first, would go to the electric chair if it came to that. She thought a lot about the electric chair, always picturing it as wood with a high, straight back, like the altar chairs at church, strung loosely with dime-store extension cords used to hook up Christmas-tree lights. And she couldn't think of the chair without remembering nights at home when the lights would flicker and somebody would say that a convict was getting electrocuted, right this very minute, at the prison in Reidsville.

When she thought about that, smelling the burned-rubber surge, tasting it hot on her tongue, she was tempted to ask Pappy Ocain how bad his bad heart was. But she wouldn't tell even if his heart was fine because then everybody would know—the truth would be out—and Pappy Ocain, all of them, would be better off dead anyway.

The trial was coming up. She didn't know the exact date and didn't care. She might be found guilty and might die, but first she'd have the baby and give it to Maude, if Maude would take it. Cliffie tried every day to trick her into promising.

Maude would come with Pappy Ocain to see Cliffie, and they would stand and talk through the bars of the new brick jail, set off by itself on the south end of the courthouse square.

"You doing awright today?" Pappy Ocain would say.

"Yessir," Cliffie'd say back, clutching the bars with her swollen hands. "How y'all doing?"

"Tolerable well," he'd say. His old head sagged like it was weighted. He would lift it with small pride, not a hint of shame that Cliffie was in jail. He could bear the shame of her

in jail better than the shame of her knowing what he knew,
what he didn't know she knew.

Maude would say, "Hum," clearing her throat and tucking
a strand of hair behind her ear. "You keeping your strength
up? You looking holler-eyed. Eat what they bring you."

"Yes 'um."

"They treating you awright?" Pappy Ocain would butt in,
his face strained, dead as he hoped his past was.

"Yessir, they good to me," Cliffie would say, and meant it,
and didn't care anyway. She'd make out till the baby came
and give it to Maude. If she'd take it.

"Mama, you reckon you can look after my baby when it
gets here?"

"Don't you be talking like that now." Maude dabbed at her
weak eyes with a handkerchief and shifted in the paisley shade
of the oak outside Cliffie's cell.

Pappy Ocain stood still, letting them woman-talk. "You
gone be out of here before you know it," said Maude.

"No 'um, I ain't, you know I ain't. You gone take care of
my baby?" Cliffie would ask again, to be sure, to make Maude
promise.

"You know I will, sugar, but . . ."

"Promise me, Mama," Cliffie'd say, fisting the bars.

"I promise." Maude would look sidelong at Pappy Ocain
and fend gnats with a roll of her thick wrist.

The fall breeze filtered through gauzy drapes of moss in
the oak and streamed through the bars, easing Cliffie's mind.
She sniffed deeply, grateful for the cool on her drawing face.

Lying on the cot, she thought of other falls, of the night
Pappy Ocain had taken everybody to the fair in Valdosta.

Roy Acuff had spied a beacon shining across the broom
sage—*Ever last one of my younguns is quick to pick up on things, specially
Cliffie*—just as the fair, which had been there two weeks, was
getting ready to move out, and he'd thought it was a flying

saucer, like the ones he'd been hearing about on the radio.

They all screamed and took on when Pappy Ocain said he'd take them to the fair—*Y'all younguns be pretty and I'll take y'all to the fair.* But he took them anyway. Loaded on the back of the pickup, like so many shoats, they'd huddled under quilts with sunned-pee batting, all twenty-or-so eyes peeled for lights across the cropped cornfields and pine woods.

The first sign of the fair came miles before they got there—blinking red and yellow spokes of the Ferris wheel turning on the black sky. They had scrambled over each other and beat on the truck hood, then hung off the sides of the pickup to gawk and wait for Pappy Ocain to make the last mile, pull up, and park.

Cliffie remembered best how he'd glanced back through the window, their delight mirrored on his face, candy-apple red in the dash light.

On such outings, an extra child or ten tagged along; anybody who would entrust their children to Pappy Ocain was welcome to send them. Say what you will, but Ocain's as good a man as they is in this county, people would say, which should have been a clear sign that it was being said comparatively. Cliffie had never noticed—or maybe she'd thought people went on like that because Pappy Ocain was poor. Not noticed till now. How she'd heard a thousand times Mr. Tinion idle up on the front porch, spit, and say, Teat told me to stop by and see if you'd get on over there, first chaince you get. But that would have been about Roy Harris, not about Pappy Ocain and Teat.

Something else: something earlier, more telling, when Cliffie was little, when she would stand and stare out at Aunt Teat's shack from her place on the truck seat. Pappy Ocain would be gone so long while Cliffie waited, stiff-kneed, cut off from the truth and the wintry wind by the windshield spattered with chicken shit. If she'd thought about anything while Pappy Ocain checked on Aunt Teat, she'd thought about that piece of Mary Jane candy he had promised if she'd be pretty till he got back.

Cliffie remembered the sneaky business of their low talk as they would finally wander from the shotgun house and stand on the stoop, Aunt Teat smiling with her hands locked behind, and Pappy Ocain dallying, then taking quick young strides to the truck. Aunt Teat waving bye, then watching the truck out of sight. And Pappy Ocain making good on his word by stopping by Hoot Walters's for candy before going on to the house, with a promise of another Mary Jane the next time and the next. If she was pretty . . .

Looking back now, Cliffie knew that allowances had been made for Pappy Ocain's past, by Maude, by everybody, because of his break with it. What Brother Leroy called his conversion: Brother Ocain's a man's been took to the limits of pleasure and pain. Cliffie found she could forgive Pappy Ocain too, would protect him too. Pray God he never knew that she knew the truth about the legacy he'd left to trap her. But she couldn't help wondering sometimes if there was not some way to get around telling and still go free, if there wasn't some way out. How bad would the town come down on her if they knew the rest? Brother Leroy had said . . .

"Our Father, who art in Heaven," she prayed, mumbling the old standby while her heart prayed on its own. Praying was all she had, a measure of peace. But she felt so sad, however peaceful, sitting and waiting and dreading the baby.

Sometimes she had to be so still, like now, sitting on the hard cot in her cell. Feeling the breeze, she mentally closed her eyes to search for something to think back on. Only through a sense of nostalgia . . .

Acorns rained on the jail roof from an overhanging branch of the oak, and she could hear them at the house, tapping on the tin roof. She lay back and daydreamed to the roll and thunk of acorns on the ground. Always daydreaming, never present; yesterday more present than today, and tomorrow always predictable and close. Little and big things alike more satisfying behind or coming up. Even the promised Mary Jane candy had tasted sweeter than the piece she was eating.

But she couldn't feel that way about the baby; she knew the present stage, with the baby stirring inside, was the best it would ever be.

Will you take care of my baby, Mama?

Yeah, honey.

No matter what?

No matter what.

All the things you want or think you want when things are going good don't seem important when you've been through the worst, waiting for the end.

Pacing the length of the cell, she wondered if the slow, rolling throb of the baby was normal. Oh, she knew the baby might not be born normal, had already accepted that. But maybe all babies behave the same before you see them, before you see whether they're normal or not. She knew how blessed it was to not see the baby but only feel it. She knew what a blessing was—to recognize a blessing *now*—and that was a blessing in itself.

All the little things that seemed important before were unimportant now: Roy Harris, Mary Helen, Fort Bragg. She still wore the ring on a string around her neck, only because it went with the baby, an unfulfilled promise, hope. Nothing really to do with Roy Harris. She was glad he was gone.

He'd be back for the trial, he had said. Maybe he'd somehow convinced Mary Helen that if she stuck to his story she could go with him to Fort Bragg then. She probably said she would—anything for love and a ticket out of town. Cliffie feared as much for Mary Helen as for herself, more for the baby Mary Helen might have someday. If he came back.

Oh, God, somebody should have killed Roy Harris; he was like a mad dog that bit everybody he bumped into. Why

hadn't somebody already shot him? Sometimes she almost
wished Pappy Ocain was like he used to be, when he still
had his trigger finger. He would have shot Roy Harris. But
that was one of the very things she protected Pappy Ocain
from, from going back. And Roy Harris was why he'd shot
off his finger in the first place. That's what Brother Leroy
had said.

He'd come to tell her everything before he left because he
had to, said he couldn't leave without her knowing what she
really faced. All of it. Now the pieces fit together to make the
ugliest picture.

He had driven up in his drab green Studebaker, packed to
the roof, a chicken-wire bird trap on top that flammed as the
car dipped in ruts. Rolled quilts and blankets, on top of cardboard boxes, stuck from each side of the open trunk.

The two children sat in the back, inert faces paler in the
bluish fall light, squeezed between cardboard boxes of egg-
beaters and mended pots and junk Christmas gifts from the
church. A Santa Claus candle with the red of the hood bleeding onto the white face, a gilt-framed needlepoint of "Home
Sweet Home," a blown-glass Coca-Cola bottle, filled with red
water; a bunch of fuzzy cattails, the shade of the children's
hair.

Sister Mary, bogged serenely in the front seat, looked
straight ahead. She'd waited before. She'd wait. It's what she
did, what she'd married to do, to sit and muse and be cruci-
fied.

The children looked cold, and Cliffie would always think
of winter and flu, smell camphorated oil, when she thought
of them—somewhere between Maude's stringy-tough brood
and Aunt Teat's crippled babies.

Cliffie's baby stood a good chance of being born like Aunt
Teat's. That's another thing Brother Leroy came to tell before
he left town.

He came bearing his black Bible like a cross: short, labored strides across the gravel side road, face leached, wounded with knowing, and lifting as he sorted Cliffie's face from the shadows. All of them waiting out there in the car, waiting while he told her, as though time was the same before and after.

Before-the-news and after-the news, that was the only time she'd ever know now, why she clung so to nostalgia, in order to go on till the baby could be born and she could witness whether its legs would fatten and kick or wither and drag.

Oh, God! Only before and after, no time between.

Mama, will you look out for my baby?

How come you to think I wouldn't? It's my duty.

"It's my duty to tell you the truth," Brother Leroy had said, after he'd been let in, brushed his feet, and stumbled over miles of meaningless amenities.

"How you been getting along?" he said.

"Pretty good," she said, staring down at her hands on the drab olive dress Maude had whipped up to cover her daughter's shame.

"I figgered I'd come before we left and say good-bye." He pulled up the only chair in the cell and sat, facing her on the cot.

She expected him to start preaching about her lying and causing so much trouble: his troubles, her own troubles, murder maybe. "I see y'all packed up to leave," she said, straining to look around him at the car chock-full of their accumulations, charity, pay. "Where y'all moving to?" She didn't care really; she focused on a seam of mortar in the red brick rows at her side. She'd found she could arrange the bricks in patterns if she tried—squares, rectangles, octagonals, straight lines, a cross, even a circle, which took some doing. It was at the point when she put together the pattern of the cross that she was forced to tread mentally backward in order to go on—to breathe and move.

"Roy Harris Weeks ain't really no Weeks—he made that up," Brother Leroy said bluntly. "He's a Flowers."

"A Flowers?" she said, feeling her scalp heat and tingle; a maze formed on the wall.

"Look at me, Cliffie!"

She concentrated on the cross of bricks, now forming.

"Look at me!" he said again. "I ain't got no reason for saying none of this but to tell you the truth. It's my duty. I tried before, I couldn't. That's how come me to try to get you to do away with the baby. Don't you think that tore me up?"

"He's kin to me, right?" She stared hard at the preacher's face, set against the evening light.

His eyes dropped. "He's your half-brother."

She thought the door slammed. Her ears rang. Somebody shouted shrilly; it was her. "My half-brother?"

"Yes, your half-brother, Brother Ocain's youngun by Teat."

"By Teat."

"Yes . . . daddy to half the flatwoods . . . a long time ago, before he got saved."

"Saved?" She couldn't recall the definition of the word, had been raised on it like cane syrup and grits. "Does he, Roy Harris, does he know?"

"Yes, he don't care." Brother Leroy gazed off. "I've come this far, I got to go on."

She saw the truth in his bleached, crying eyes and decided not to call him a liar. His face took on hot patches of pink, as from a red reflection, tender lips muttering again that he had to go on.

The car still sat there, hood glinting in the blue-yellow lightfall. Equinox had passed. Resurrection, life and death. Withering for winter. A drumroll of acorns sounded overhead. Cliffie could smell her own sweat, wood smoke somewhere. The cell she'd thought of as temporary became death row at Reidsville. No longer familiar Cornerville beyond the bars, where Highway 129 was being paved, north to south. Roads didn't lead anywhere.

"I've got to tell you because you can get off clean if you decide to tell it." Head bowed, he went on. "I don't know if even your mama knows everything. Brother Ocain confessed his sins to me, not just to the Lord, like I tried to get him to. And confession is privileged—private. It's against everything I stand for to tell even you."

"Tell me," she said, gritting her teeth and feeling sick hatred well inside.

"It gets real bad." He got up and paced to the bars, as though to check on the car and his waiting, his used-to-waiting family. "If I was you I'd leave things like they are. Let everybody think it's my baby, that the house got accidentally set afire. But that's got to be up to you.

"I've spent my whole life, since I was called, trying to live up to what I promised, and now. . . . " His voice trailed off, quavering, as he polished rust from a bar with one holy white hand. "Roy Harris is plain evil, through and through, crazy, according to psychology. He's a good six to eight years older than he claims."

"Pappy Ocain and Aunt Teat?" Cliffie said, still hoping for something and she didn't know what.

"Teat was a good old soul. Too good." He rubbed the bar, up and down and around, then ground it with his fist. "Used to be right attractive, they say."

Cliffie cradled her arms, rocking, and watched his too-short blue suit sleeve riding up his arm.

His voice came tight and expectant, a bad riddle. "You know how come Brother Ocain to shoot off his trigger finger?"

"So he wouldn't shoot nobody else," Cliffie said.

"So he wouldn't shoot Roy Harris."

"Why?"

"For raping Teat."

Cliffie closed him out with crying, and when she could see

again, hear again, he was standing over her, holding a wet cloth to her brow.

"You had to know," he whispered, voice raspy as though he'd been crying too.

"The dead children . . . ?"

"Probably was his," he finished.

He let her cry, still pressing the cloth to her forehead, right hand clamped in an anointing on her crown. She wailed till she thought her ears would burst. He tucked the damp hair at her temples behind her ears.

"Please say it ain't so," she begged.

"I can't," he said. "I wish I could. Brother Ocain disowned him a long time ago."

"Why didn't she kill him?" Cliffie tilted back on the cot, sucking in.

"Because she loved him," Brother Leroy said softly. "She didn't have the heart to have him locked up again. She'd sent him off to reform school in Jacksonville before. Didn't solve nothing. She was ignorant, Cliffie, but she was good. He, Roy Harris, roughed her up pretty bad one time, and she come to me. I was all to pieces. Her lip was busted, she smelt of blood, and me wishing I could look off. In a little while, she said, 'Look, least I ain't dead,' got up and went home.

"I've seen that old woman stronger at her weakest than most people at their best, and I've seen her pull the wool over more eyes—Brother Ocain's included—in getting where she had to go; not to try to take nothing weren't coming to her anyway, but to take what they had to give before they could hand it out, as a matter of pride: a little bit of power she could lord over everybody. The church should of been the one place she was on level ground, nose to nose, with everybody. And I don't know . . . we come close."

"What about Mary Helen?"

"Yes." He stiffened. "I know about her, too; I can't help her. But Roy Harris won't come back, you can rest easy. And she'll be all right. The next boy comes along . . . Roy Harris won't never show up at Fort Bragg—rats don't have much sense of direction, just instincts.

"I'm telling you all this so you can choose to defend yourself or let it go. I'd stay with the story about the accident if I was you and about it being my baby. Mary even wonders if it ain't mine now."

Cliffie shrank.

"She'll be all right." Brother Leroy sighed. "And don't worry much about being sent off: they're good people around here, for the most part. I've seen 'em lash out at Aunt Teat because looking at her made them feel guilty. They couldn't stand being reminded of what-all went on with her and Roy Harris: a blight on all they hold good, on the town. Yeah, they know about him, and I doubt they place much confidence in what he had to say about the fire. They're just upset over the babies and Aunt Teat getting burnt up. Speaking from experience, it's easier to look the other way than to look at Roy Harris—maybe even easier to look at you. But they judge from the heart more than reason. I'd take a chance on them. They're people with mercy running in their veins. A lot more innocent than ignorant—there's a difference."

"You're leaving," Cliffie said.

"Not 'cause they made me," he said, eyes melty. He stroked her hair like a lover, with a glazed look of being at last set free from suspicious eyes. "I don't have to leave, but like Brother Ocain said, it's better the town believe it's me the daddy of your baby than Roy Harris . . ."

"Pappy Ocain *does* know," Cliffie said.

"From the very first," said the preacher, wheeling slowly to look away. "Out in the woods that day, he come right face-to-face with me, and I'd done decided he could shoot me dead, but I wouldn't tell what you told me. He looked me right in the eye and said, 'Lord God in heaven!' then shot straight up like he was shooting at God . . ."

"Then he told you?"

"He just went on, all mixed up, about how he'd brung such a thing on you with his tomcatting around."

Cliffie started to cry again, and the preacher waited, then said, "Me and him come to the decision that they wadn't no way out but me—me and you. For me to leave and let everybody think I messed you up. The town knows about Brother Ocain's past, wouldn't never let you live it down if they suspicioned your baby was Roy Harris's. Brother Ocain don't want you to know that shame, his shame—specially you, Cliffie. And one more mouth to feed, one more youngun on Maude wouldn't be no more hardship."

Cliffie made a strangled sound. "Maybe I should of got rid of it." She didn't mean it.

"No," Brother Leroy broke in, "Brother Ocain didn't never say that, wouldn't even think that way. I was wrong, you were right. Everybody's got a right to be born, live, and die. They all give something . . ."

"Like Aunt Teat's babies."

"Yes—even Roy Harris."

"I don't think so."

"He gave you a baby. Born good or bad, could be the only life you ever get the chance to give."

"I love it."

"Teat loved hers."

"But what if my baby . . . ?" Cliffie cried evenly, face tilted as she rocked. "My baby, it'll be . . ."

"Maybe not," he said, both knowing it could be born deformed. Quite likely would be. Neither said it.

He leaned down and hugged her, his arms warm through the scratchy suit coat, and began to pray, loud, with his bony chin on her head. Sun standing still over the jail, he prayed that her baby would be born normal, that she'd be all right, that somehow the whole mess would come clean. When he'd prayed until the words no longer came, he stood, oblivious of the world that was welcome to peep through the bars. "It'll be born anyway, the baby will," he said. "With or without you telling."

"Yes," she said, feeling the baby stir, safe in not knowing yet.

The sun, now striking the hood of the car from a westerly slant, reflected on the red brick wall behind and shone in her eyes. "It was a accident," she said.

In no hurry, he pulled the chair nearer and placed both his hands on her knees. His eyes unblinking, his face dry and splotchy. He kissed her on the cheek, a brotherly kiss.

She touched his face, then let her hand drop back to her lap, tried to smile but couldn't. Words came spilling out, and she told him what had really happened, sparing nothing, telling it until dusk, until his blue eyes brimmed with grief and foreknowing. She told it for the first and last time and told him to go, to take it with him. "It was a accident, as far as anybody else needs to know."

"Yes," he said. "I'll go."

"I'm sorry," she said. "I'm so ashamed of myself."

"We're all ashamed of ourselfs." He turned and strolled out, without once looking back.

She stood and crossed the cell, watching him stroll to the car, watching Sister Mary and the children, immutably still, their stillness resounding in the brattle of gravel as they drove away, taking Cliffie's secret over the Alapaha bridge and beyond the little-town line.

The first time Pappy Ocain actually set foot inside Cliffie's cell, he simply followed the sheriff in with Cliffie's supper, both of them fumbling and fiddling with the door, as if one was waiting for the other to shut it, Pappy Ocain holding a sprig of pink crepe myrtle, the oversized sheriff holding an aluminum dinner tray.

The sheriff sidled awkwardly over to Cliffie's cot, looking

back at Pappy Ocain, not that he had any notion the old man might try something, but because he looked so out of place inside, always hung around the door like a dog waiting for scraps. The sheriff placed the tray on Cliffie's lap. "Pull up that chair yonder, Ocain, and set down," he said, lifting the soggy wax paper from the tray. "If I'd knowed you was coming I'd of had Orlean send you over some supper too. Chicken and dumplings."

He rimmed his blue uniform collar with his finger and went back to the door, stepped beyond the threshold of concrete and gravel, and turned. "When you get done, Ocain, how 'bout shutting this door for me?" Then he lumbered off around the corner to the blind side of the cell.

"I knowed that boy of C.W.'s would make a fine sheriff," Pappy Ocain said. "All heart." He sat in the chair before Cliffie and twirled the sprig of crepe myrtle, knuckles, kneecaps, nose, and ears backlit by the evening light.

Cliffie tasted the chicken and dumplings, a stringy gelatinous mixture, then picked at the banana pudding, at the clean divide where the dipping spoon had cut through the vanilla wafers.

Toes together, Pappy Ocain bounced his heels. He seemed to notice his jittering feet and slid them flat before him. "I love you, gal, I just love you. I don't know what-all you done or what-all's been done to you, but I love you all the same. And I'll be right here till me or you one lays down and dies."

He didn't mean *stay in the cell*—she didn't think he meant that. She didn't know till he stayed.

He handed her the flower and sat back with his hairy hands spread on his thighs. Again, his heels started to spring and jitter. He groaned deep inside and started to cry.

"Don't cry, Pappy Ocain," she said, not looking at his face to see. "Please don't. What about your bad heart?"

Crying and shaking, he sounded like a hurt dog. "I'd walk right out that door there and tell ery man come by that that's my girl youngun in jail yonder. I'd say it to Abe Guess, or Mr. Anybody, 'Yessir, and ain't we all made mistakes? Ain't we all done bad we wish we could undo?'" His voice thickened with the dusk at his back.

Cliffie cried too, without sound, glad her eyes were weepy anyway. She dabbed them, swallowed hard. "It's okay, Pappy Ocain. I always knowed you loved me."

"I didn't go to love you so hard, baby."

"You didn't." She choked, coughed.

He cried openly, lips stretched across those painted-on teeth he'd worn just for her. "I made so many messes in this old world, enough for ten men . . ."

"Don't talk about it, Pappy Ocain," she said, praying he wouldn't tell about Teat and Roy Harris, about fathering half the flatwoods, that she wouldn't tell him that she knew he knew. If they said it all, too many words would be loosed ever to be bound. If they brought out in the open what they both knew, the truth would be too much of a lie to lay honestly before the court.

"I didn't come here to make it no worse on you," he said, blowing his nose, a terrible rending of the somber, always somber, cell, "to get shed of my own guilt. When I got saved Brother Leroy told me that by the Bible my sins was scattered east to west and buried in the deepest seas. I want you to know that. When the Lord put us here he knowed we weren't perfect—just One was. We s'posed to try to be."

"Yessir." She knew he'd come to tell everything and was afraid if he did she'd have to leave on the new road opening in Cornerville, that if the town knew about her and Roy Harris she couldn't stay. But she knew she couldn't go; all roads circled back. "If you done confessed to God, don't think no more about it, Pappy Ocain."

"You right," he said, groaning deep and blowing. "That'd be digging up a old bone. I just come here to say I love you and I love your little baby, don't matter who the daddy is. And me and your ma'll take care of it." He cried louder, buried his face in the crook of his arm.

A leathery brown toad hopped through the door, across the floor. *Don't come in here, don't come in here!* Cliffie felt like screaming. She cried openly now, her always-weeping eyes weeping with reason. "Don't cry, Pappy Ocain, you'll make yourself sick." She got up and put her arms around his sloped shoulders and kissed his feverish face. He shook all over. He clutched her head and held it firm against his. "I oughta take you on to the house, gal."

"I can't go, Pappy Ocain."

The frog hopped to a corner and puffed up, went down.

"I don't know how anybody could believe a fine girl like you could set a house afire with them babies in it. Teat . . ."

"No, Pappy Ocain," Cliffie clamped a hand over his mouth, felt his rubbery gums working. She waited a long time before taking her hand away, for the frog to spring from the corner, for it to hop across the slick concrete and out the door.

Then she lay down, holding to Pappy Ocain's hand, and knew they were both safe, that the closest he'd come to mentioning Roy Harris was the night of the fire—*I mought as well set fire to your big toe, gal*—and the fire Pappy Ocain set was the dare she took with Roy Harris. Pappy Ocain knew because she was just like him.

Somewhere in the long night she slept and dreamed of hopping from the cell and slamming the door to find that all of Cornerville was burning, flames shooting from the courthouse, the post office, the health department, Hoot's store, all the women—only women—running with their clothes on fire across the intersection where the traffic light was set to blink on red. Her clothes caught fire, then her hair, but she felt no pain, felt resigned to burning, as she watched the other women—Aunt Teat, Maude, Mary Helen, Emmacee, Pee-Jean,

Sister Mary, the postmistress, the county nurse, and the women from the churches—dash screaming up the new 129 and circle back at Troublesome Creek, faces black as Witch Seymour's.

The slide, rattle, and clank of the door jolted her awake. Her hand numb in Pappy Ocain's grip, he reared back, sleeping with his mouth gaped. The big sheriff, standing just inside with the breakfast tray, looked at them, then turned to rattle Pappy Ocain awake with the door. "Orlean sent you some hoecakes and syrup this morning," he said to Cliffie. "Thought you might could do with a change, some sweetening." Then to Pappy Ocain, "If I'd knowed you was gone still be here, Ocain, I'd of had her fix you a plate."

Cliffie could see the cars and trucks as they slowed on the new black pavement, could hear them pull up and park on the gravel borders of the courtyard, and found herself listening hard for traffic from the north and east, blind sides of her cell. She shivered, thinking of all those people coming just to see her tried.

She'd thought she was over worrying about her looks, but now she pictured her face, pictured the face of the crowd, and loved her cell she'd set up like home: a table made from a cardboard box beside her cot with a black miniature New Testament—the one the Gideon people gave out at school—and Pappy Ocain's dead sprig of pink crepe myrtle, the shade of a virgin's dried blood.

Archie Wall, Cliffie's lawyer, had warned her that, if the jury found her guilty of what she kept calling *a accident*, she could be on her way to prison following the trial.

She hooked both hands on the cool bars and squeezed. On what she now thought of as her porch, the front half of the cell, she exercised her fingers every day, to loosen the webby skin, but now she squeezed the bars to relax. She dreaded walking the concrete trail through the courtyard, past the sheriff's office, to the new brick courtroom facing the main intersection of Cornerville.

Except for weekly visits to the health-department clinic, across the gravel road, she hadn't set foot outside her cell. And somehow the thrust of her tight, round stomach had seemed hidden from Maude and her brothers when they stopped by, as though the bars were a solid wall they all talked through. Crossing the road with the sheriff to the clinic, she would look back at the walk that ran between the two brick wings of the courthouse and dread the trial.

Now that she knew she would recover from the burns, that the baby could be born deformed, now that she'd take jail over freedom to keep from telling, she was reconciled to everything. Yet, in a way, getting better had made her self-conscious again about facing everybody on court day, and she felt wistful for even the old stinging pain when at least she'd been peacefully reconciled to only the horror of pain. Because following horror there is hope, and she didn't want to hope anymore. She didn't want to dread going to the courtroom for everybody to pity and judge.

She dabbed at her eyes with the handkerchief Maude had left for her. Everybody would think she was crying, her spirits broken, and really she was all right. Left alone, she was fine. She cocked her head and listened to feet scurrying along the concrete walk, coming closer, and her heart started to race.

"It's come time, Cliffie," said the sheriff, rounding the blind side of the cell with Archie Wall. The sheriff's pure blue eyes looked odd in his horsy face, eyes always looking beyond her, as if to look at her he'd have to look away or let her go or look inside himself. He was abnormally tall, and she so short—could walk right under his arm. But to think of him looking the other way and letting her go was ridiculous. His power. Her impotence. In his line of work he couldn't afford to look inside, Cliffie decided, and felt close to him. And if

she *should* run, what would he do? where would she go? There
was really no way out of town for Cliffie, no way out of the
body, soul, and mind of Cliffie—pain had taught her that. If
she *could* catch a ride on one of the semis parked down the
street at the café, where would she end up and how would
she manage with a deformed baby? She had to stay close to
Maude. The sheriff had seemed to read her mind and had quit
locking the cell door weeks ago.

Cliffie was moved that the sheriff trusted her. She never
touched the place on the door frame where she could so easily slide the door back. She watched the handhold, rubbed
shiny as a dime on the rust above the square lock, and
thought about touching it but never did. And Pappy Ocain
came and went as he pleased, and sometimes he stayed all
night, sitting up in the chair by her cot as he did the first
time. The sheriff knew, and Cliffie suspected that was the real
reason the door was left unlocked.

Archie Wall, the only lawyer in Swanoochee County, stood
beside the cell door while the sheriff slid it aside, a slight
grating, as though neither could *he*, Archie Wall, touch the
legally shut door. "Cliffie, how you?" he said, bobbed his
small round head and held his hands.

With the door open, Cliffie felt naked. She wished it
would close, wished they'd go away and let her go on serving
time here, from this day on. Once she'd told Archie Wall that
and he had said, But, gal, that ain't how the system works.
And she'd said, But it should if you don't want nothing
changed; the other way round, say, if you wanted to get out,
that would be different. I don't.

Did you do it, gal? he asked—just that once.

In a way, yessir, she said. *It was a accident.*

You want to go over anything on Roy Harris Weeks?

It was a accident.

That ain't much to go on.

No sir; it's all I got.

And he acted as if he knew what she was talking about, being the lawyer in Swanoochee County everybody used—they'd pay him when they could—where nobody trusted the law anymore than the church, though everybody believed. Maybe, like Brother Leroy, he'd stayed in Cornerville because he'd just as soon look to people with mercy running in their veins as those outside with cold blood and mingled whim.

"They're waiting over yonder." Archie Wall nodded toward the courtroom and stepped back, his little feet mincing on the gravel like a donkey's. His legs were thin, his belly popped round, the buttons of his court-worn white shirt straining at the holes.

Stepping outside, Cliffie's lips tingled in the blast of cold air, and she could have sworn that the wall of bars was solid after all.

The sheriff started to bend and take her elbow but stepped back, letting her walk ahead. Self-consciously, he took off his hat and raked his fingers through his scatter of reddish hair.

Cliffie, having seen the sheriff blush red to his collar, and having even hated him a little at first, wished she could be by herself with him—back to normal. "Y'all seen Pappy Ocain and my mama this pretty morning?" Walking along, she thought the word "pretty" sounded impossible but necessary to round off a level sort of cheeriness, which she didn't feel but which made the two men more at ease and set for herself a mood.

"I seen 'em going in the courtroom a while ago," the sheriff said, shuffling behind Archie Wall.

The sheriff always walked with long, uncertain strides but had learned to take short steps for Cliffie, and the difference between strides served well to justify their awkwardness together when she went over to the clinic and spread her legs, heels hooked into cold metal stirrups—a sort of rape—while the sheriff stood outside the door.

Through the wall of jalousie windows she could see the crowded courtroom. "Archie Wall, your indigestion any better?"

"'Bout straightened out," he said, shuffling behind.

She looked up at their reflection in a closed window and smiled: both she and Archie Wall short and round, paunches going first.

Somebody in the courtroom, behind the next turned-out window, whispered, "Look at that! Her just a-smiling."

Cliffie wiped her eyes and looked down to step up at the crosswalk, then up at the open double doors of the burbling courtroom. The crowd parted in the breezeway, the throng in the doorway making room for Cliffie to pass, every wall lined, every bench filled in the broad room, musty though airy with light.

She strained to avoid faces as she walked up the aisle, peering down at khaki and green twill pants legs, plaid skirts, and dark, dusty shoes, sandals with dirty toes. Halfway to the front, she spied a new pair of black ballerinas and stopped. Her gaze traveled from the shoes to the face. "Mary Helen," she said.

Her sister's slack lips hardened; she stared straight ahead, as if she dared not associate with such.

Cliffie walked on, thinking about how much Mary Helen had wanted those shoes, how she'd tried on Dottie Jean Belt's at the Twin Lakes Pavilion. Backed into a booth, she'd crossed her legs on the bench to admire the black leather molds of her feet.

Lonesome for old times—for her pretty self, even lonesome for Mary Helen—Cliffie could see the tender pink puckers of scars on her own nose and cheeks when she looked down.

"She used to be right attractive," somebody whispered. "The best-looking one of Ocain's bunch."

"Yeah, and ain't he taking it hard, gone downhill till it's a sight."

She used to be right attractive—what Brother Leroy had said about Aunt Teat.

Cliffie, teetering in the aisle, felt dazed. Archie Wall sidestepped around and led her to the front, to a pine table on the left, which faced a podium like the one at church. He pulled out a chair for her to sit, then collapsed in the one beside and blew as if he were bushed.

Barely turning her head, Cliffie scanned the crowd for Pappy Ocain. He was sitting with Maude and the children in the front row of the right side, the boys all scrunched, from K.C. in the middle to Scooter on the end. Cliffie smiled; Pappy Ocain smiled, then trained his eyes ahead. Quacker buried her face in Maude's lap. Cliffie wondered if the children were shocked by her face. She hoped maybe they hadn't recognized her with her chin shrunk, face grained and drawn, bottom row of teeth shining. The doctor who had promised to fix her face had said he'd do it later, and she knew that welfare patients had to wait.

Archie Wall had warned her that the trial could last three days. Three days! She stared at the wall of port-wine brick behind the judge's bench and was glad for something familiar, started trying to conjure images, as she had in her cell. But it was no use. She was too distracted by Emmacee Mae and the others whispering the whole time the jury was being selected.

Almost everybody called for jury duty from the church in the flatwoods got turned down by Archie Wall. Hiking his low-riding gray trousers, he came down on each, until one by one they were eliminated. When Tinion Culpepper was seated in the witness chair—before Archie Wall could open his mouth to ask if he had any preconceived notions—the old deacon burst out, "Ocain ain't got nary girl youngun would

NECESSARY LIES ▌ 151

set fire to a *dog*." Tinion stood for emphasis, lit green eyes scanning for effect. Everybody started to talk, the judge pounded the gavel, and Archie Wall said he'd take Tinion and eleven more like him.

The District Attorney laughed, smooth and mellifluous, rocking back in his chair, and from there tried to oust Tinion, but the judge let him stay. The judge said, "Don't ask me how come," and everybody laughed.

Tinion moped over to the empty jury box and sat peering curiously around. Archie Wall strutted across the front of the courtroom, called the next prospective juror from memory, and eliminated him. Then he weakened.

At one point during the long morning, while the yellow sun filled every window and shed over Cliffie and Archie Wall, she heard him snoring, him reared in the chair with his fleshy arms drawn to the sides.

The District Attorney, a handsome, clear-faced man, seemed to take all the time in the world, as if he could buy more if that ran out. Nobody ever referred to him as other than Mr. *District Attorney*. Occasionally, while he questioned prospective jurors, Cliffie wouldn't know exactly what he meant, and then again she would sense what was meant but could never explain, even to herself, what he was driving at. But she knew she was being slurred and knew it wasn't personal, just par for the legal process.

"Would you call yourself a man of God, Mr. Walters?" he asked.

Hoot bowed his chest and tilted his face. "I do my derndest to."

A few people laughed along the front, titters scattering to the banked spectators at the door. "'I do my derndest,'" they mimicked proudly.

"Sir, would you be able to render a fair and honest assessment of the case before us?"

"You mean if I believed Cliffie there burnt up Aunt Teat and them babies could I send her off?" Hoot sat forward, shimming his fingers. "Yes sir, I could."

"Mr. Wall." The District Attorney turned smartly, polished black shoes clicking to the table aligned with Archie Wall's. He was smiling to himself, an all-purpose smile.

At that point, that smile could have been because poor old Archie Wall—whom everybody made fun of for being dumb enough to believe he was smart enough to be a lawyer—had been caught dozing. But later on the District Attorney still smiled that way when Archie Wall pointed out that Cliffie hadn't been "hog-tied" to Aunt Teat's back porch during the fire, that she could have left and not been burned herself. He turned one hand out, to present the victim, paused, then picked up where he had left off. "Somebody else strung the kerosene, somebody else struck the match." Archie Wall stalked back to his table and sat, almost steaming in the blare of sunshine.

"No sir," Cliffie hissed, shaking his arm. "If you go and do that again, I won't go through with this."

"You have to, girl." He gazed off, his slick, round face so dumb it could go for smart. "That's how the system works."

"It was a accident," Cliffie said, "and don't you go trying to make it something else."

"Roy Harris was there somewhere."

"I done told you I don't want his name brung up."

Just as Brother Leroy had predicted, Roy Harris hadn't shown up at Fort Bragg. Archie Wall said he'd been summoned to testify, then seemingly had been forgotten. Cliffie would have to bring him up or nobody would. She knew that, preferred that.

When court reconvened after lunch, Cliffie, paraded in, again felt self-conscious. But later, with her back to the spectators, she settled into the proceedings, sometimes dozing with

Archie Wall, sometimes listening to the smooth and eloquent voice of the District Attorney, out of tone in Swanoochee County, almost thinking of the case as applying to someone else. Someone else even carrying the baby, someone else scarred and maimed, someone else sitting at the defendants' table with Archie Wall, whom she'd never made fun of but thought of as funny.

Staring out the window, around three o'clock, she watched the yellow school buses crawl along the shortcut that ran two blocks from the school to the jail, feeling in the air the cool midafternoon stasis of mid-October, and forgot who she was and why she was there, almost believing that this tedious process could go on tediously and statically forever, and she would stay just as she was, not even taking a break to birth the baby or watch Pappy Ocain's sapped face or go to prison, where the electric chair waited.

Thinking about the electric chair always brought her around. And she'd go back through wondering how bad Pappy Ocain's bad heart was, how bad it would be for the whole town to know the baby was Roy Harris's, how bad for Pappy Ocain to know she knew that he knew, and whether she could afford to tell, could afford not to tell.

Pappy Ocain blew his nose and, recognizing the sound, Cliffie turned to look at him: elbows on knees, tilted out from Maude and the three smallest children, who napped on and around, covering Maude. Liver spots blotched her pale face.

Cliffie smiled.

Maude wagged her head, as if to say, It'll all come out in the wash. Cliffie wondered if that was what Maude's look meant, had been wondering a lot lately: Maude had to know something.

Cliffie sat up straight. She had to turn slightly to look square at Maude and, in so doing, caught everybody's collective eye. Cliffie felt her face burn. She couldn't take her eyes off Maude, whose eyes were riveted on her.

She knows, Cliffie thought. I don't know how she knows, but she knows. Oh, God! Her mama's knowing didn't change a thing, but knowing she knew changed everything. Had Cliffie thought that her mama was so wrapped up in babies and oblivious that she wouldn't know the truth if it walked up and slapped her? Or maybe that Maude, being an outsider by blood and circumstance, wouldn't be privy to the town's secrets? Maybe both. Maybe more: that Maude, the sow, was a fool. But even fools have ears, even sows have instincts. Maude looked so instinctive, sitting now in the midst of her litter, that den of her own undoing.

Pappy Ocain stuffed his handkerchief into his hip pocket and sat back, arm going automatically around Maude's shoulders. Her eyes were still on Cliffie, like beams in a dark room.

Cliffie stared at her hands in a deep study.

Sitting in the courtroom the next morning, in the bubblelike refractory of light, Cliffie still sat in a deep study, still staring at her hands. If Maude knew about Pappy Ocain and Teat, the crippled babies, why hadn't she said something to Cliffie?

She had. She'd said it over and over, when she'd said how bad Pappy Ocain's heart was. A warning?

Jury selection done, the District Attorney called his first witness. "The State calls Master K.C. Flowers," he said.

Everybody shuffled and mumbled.

K.C. loped from the second row, behind Pappy Ocain, swung up on the witness stand and plopped. Rubbing his nose and stalling, he looked everywhere but at the District Attorney, who started out kind but gradually got sarcastic. At one point, he waved a half-circle, implying that maybe the boy was a mite daft, and everybody laughed, bringing K.C. out of his stupor.

Sometimes the smooth-talking District Attorney would ask K.C. a question and he'd look dumb and swing his feet, and the District Attorney, seeing he was getting nowhere, would rephrase the question so K.C. could answer correctly with either a simple yes or no.

"Are you brother to the defendant?"

"Yes sir."

"Are you twelve years old?"

"Yes sir."

"Were you out at the church pumphouse on the evening of August 21?"

"I don't know," K.C. said, peeping up at Cliffie.

"Now, Master Flowers," the District Attorney said, going quickly on. "Tell us what the defendant—your sister, Cliffie Flowers—said on the evening of the fire when she ran from the church toward the woods."

K.C. sat forward, suddenly aiming for honesty with sling-shot words. "I can't swear it *was* Cliffie. Us boys was jabbering and spitting water . . ."

"Master K.C., didn't you specify initially that it *was* Cliffie, the defendant, who said—and I quote for the record and for the express purpose of piquing the memory of this young man—'I'm gone kill that devil?'"

"Sir?"

The District Attorney, composed but pacing, broke the question down.

"Yes sir, I said that," K.C. said, "but I give it some thought and it might not of even been Cliffie atall. She weren't the onliest one come out; Mary Helen come out just ahead of her."

That evening, back in her cell, Cliffie talked to her mama through the bars. "Mama, I told Archie Wall to tell you to come over here by yourself 'cause I need to know something."

"He told me," Maude said, fanning her face with a roll of the wrist.

It was almost dark, a steely dusk, thick with the shrieks of katydids in the oak at Maude's back.

"You get Mary Helen to take care of the babies?" Cliffie asked.

"I did."

"Where's Pappy Ocain?"

"On the porch, setting; I left him on the porch."

"He know how come I sent word for you?"

"No 'um, he don't." Maude's face was shallow, bloodless, and brave.

"But you know how come?"

"Yes 'um, I 'spect I do." When Maude was serious, down to business, she always said "yes 'um" or "no 'um," even to the children. And she wouldn't even blink.

Cliffie spoke low, in a testing voice, and in case Pappy Ocain or somebody should happen up. "You know all about me and Roy Harris and Mary Helen?"

"I do."

"You know about Pappy Ocain and . . . ?"

"And Teat. Yes 'um, I do." She fanned again, didn't blink. "Roy Harris is his'n. Emmacee Mae . . ."

"Don't tell me no more, Mama," Cliffie butted in, "just tell me Pappy Ocain don't know I know."

"He don't."

Cliffie knew Maude was chilly by the way she rubbed her wrapped arms. "Mama, come on in."

Maude hesitated, then shuffled along the bars with her head down. At the door, she stopped and brushed her feet, then slid the door open and stepped inside.

Cliffie watched her change, coming in from the dulling dusk of the outside, face plainly pained in the raw cell light. They stood looking at one another, alone for what seemed the first time.

"You know my baby's pro'bly gone be born a cripple?"

"Might could be." Maude's voice cracked; she covered her mouth—her speckled eyes misty—then just as quickly dropped her hand. "If you ask Him for a fish, will He give you a stone?" she added.

"Mama, I'm scared."

"Don't you fret." Maude reached out to her on impulse but dropped her arms. "I might not know the law, but I do know my own younguns."

"Help me, Mama." Cliffie threw her arms around Maude's neck and sank into her soft body, burrowing as though she might hide.

"I will, I will." Maude breathed into her hair, rubbed her back hard.

Cliffie pulled away and held Maude's stout shoulders. "Listen to me, Mama. I love you for what you're wanting to do for me. And I do know you'd do what you could, but don't you go and mess up. Don't tell nobody what happened, and don't tell Pappy Ocain I know. It'd kill him."

"You're pretty," Maude said, smearing a tear across Cliffie's cheek. "You're pretty where it counts."

Cliffie knew Maude meant it and felt redeemed; ugly as her face was, there was something alive within her, something pretty. "Mama, we've got to look out for Pappy Ocain. Don't you do nothing, trying to get me off."

"You're younger'n he is, honey."

And Maude stayed till night came.

On the second day of the trial, the District Attorney called Mary Helen.

Cliffie sat stiffly watching as Mary Helen, thinner and more subdued, approached the witness stand. She stepped up, turned, and stared at the Holy Bible held before her.

"Place your hand on the Bible, Mary Helen," the District Attorney said, having toned down all formalities to fit in, to reach the witnesses. He'd even taken off his fine black coat, white shirt stark in the moving streaks of sun.

"Do you solemnly swear to tell the truth, the whole truth, and nothing but the truth, so help you God?" the Clerk of the Court said.

"I do." Mary Helen looked at Maude and Pappy Ocain.

"Now, Mary Helen," the District Attorney began. He walked straight toward her, stopping short. "Where was your sister the evening of the fire?"

Mary Helen stretched her lips, chin dimpling. "She was with me."

"Wait!" he said, stepping closer to pin her with his eyes. "I thought you said you didn't know where Cliffie was but she wasn't in church."

"I might've said that. But she was right outside with me. We'd been fussing all day and we went outside church to settle it. Cliffie looked up and seen smoke and took off through the woods. Weren't long before some of the younguns at the pumphouse seen it too and run to tell everybody in church."

"I suppose you went right on with Cliffie when you *seen* smoke?"

"No sir," Mary Helen said. "I was scared to death of that crazy Roy Harris Weeks. Bad about hanging around in the woods." She rubbed her nose furiously with her fist. Then she posed in place like a dried corn stalk in fall.

"Why didn't you come forward and exonerate—free—your sister earlier? Why didn't you tell this before?"

"Uh huh, I hear you!" Mary Helen seemed caught up in her imaginings. "Roy Harris Weeks would as soon shoot you as spit on you. He'd a come back and hunted me down if I'd told." Her face stained red and she started to cry.

Cliffie turned to look at Maude; she was wagging her head, eyes knowing, afraid. Pappy Ocain sat forward.

"Miss Flowers . . . Mary Helen," the District Attorney said, undone. "Were you jealous of your sister with Roy Harris?"

She snorted, dried her eyes on the puffed sleeve of her red polka-dotted dress. "I don't know how come I would be."

"Weren't both of you going with him?"

The crowd came alive out of a dead listening strain. Cliffie felt a punch in the stomach.

"Wouldn't your sister have tried to kill him if she thought you were going with him also; say, if for instance she was pregnant with his baby?"

"Emmacee Mae tell you all that trash?" Mary Helen, white, aghast, stared beyond him to the middle row on the left where Emmacee sat mumbling.

"Answer the question."

"Not to my beknownst."

"Answer my question."

"I guess she could've."

Everybody started talking; the judge pounded on the bench. Somebody said, "Shut up! *Shut up!*"

"Stop them, Archie Wall," Cliffie whispered.

"You bald-faced, lying Mary Helen Flowers!" Emmacee hollered. "You 'bout the one set fire to the house. You! You got up and went out of the church house, bellering."

"Shut up, Emmacee!" said Mary Helen, shooting from the chair. "Me nor Cliffie nary one weren't going with that freak. We had better raising. *You* was. And we all know it was Roy Harris set fire to that house. We all know it."

Emmacee Mae stood, holding to the bench ahead, twisting and quarreling.

"Don't worry 'bout 'em," Archie Wall said behind his hand, then reared in his chair, tense and distanced. "You couldn't have a better de-fense. If the judge was to send you up now, he'd have to send everybody up. Ain't a man in this county born without a knowledge of Ocain's past, and your sister is right about one thing—they let Roy Harris give 'em the slip." He shook his head. "The preacher's name ain't once been brung up, or what-all went on out there in them woods."

He seemed to be speaking to the District Attorney now,

low and through his ground-down teeth, the way a man in danger might pray. "Man, please! Just let it go. Let it go! You ain't got no notion what you a-messing with. Don't open it up no more'n you have to. Go home."

Numbly, Cliffie watched Archie Wall's face, the dew of sweat making in the wispy tan mustache under his nose, his eyes glazing over.

The District Attorney faced the judge and said, "Somebody's been tampering with the witnesses."

The judge shook his head and waved the District Attorney away. "Mr. Wall?" the District Attorney said, face wiped clean of smiling as he sat.

"I rest my case," said Archie Wall, smiling because he had no case to rest. He didn't even stand—didn't need to—just sat with Cliffie while Mary Helen stumbled down, grumbling at Emmacee.

"Y'all go on home, Ocain," the judge said, "and take Cliffie there with you."

"These people don't go by the law," Archie Wall mumbled, "the law goes by them."

Cliffie sucked in, waited a minute, then looked back at Pappy Ocain. He sat straight, face slack with relief, but grieved.

Listening to the whispery scuffing of Mary Helen's new black ballerinas, Cliffie watched her mince across the front and down the aisle. The shoes. How did she get those shoes? She couldn't have come up with that kind of money. I don't know much about the law, but I do know my own younguns, Maude had said. Cliffie's face tingled. She knew that Mary Helen, figuring Roy Harris wouldn't be back, had sold out for a new pair of shoes, that Maude had bought them.

"Mama?" Cliffie intoned.

Maude nodded.